THE PLANT
GOD

THE PLANT
GOD

ROGER LEE VERNON

TRUE DIRECTIONS | iUniverse®
AN AFFILIATE OF TARCHER PERIGEE

The Plant God

iUniverse books may be ordered through booksellers or by contacting:

iUniverse
1663 Liberty Drive
Bloomington, IN 47403
www.iuniverse.com
1-800-Authors (1-800-288-4677)

ISBN: 978-1-4917-9795-2 (sc)
ISBN: 978-1-4917-9794-5 (hc)
ISBN: 978-1-4917-9793-8 (e)

Library of Congress Control Number: 2016908545

Print information available on the last page.

iUniverse rev. date: 06/24/2016

CONTENTS

PROLOGUE

So much had already happened, the love story, the adventure tale, the chase, the great puzzle, and all will be told soon, but for now we start in the middle looking next at the wilder past and then the even more amazing future.

1

PREPARING FOR INTERPLANETARY WAR

Andy Mars wandered through the narrow twisting streets of the Grand Bazaar of the old city. He was a stranger here in a dangerous land, and therefore alert, his senses sharpened, his mental antenna out, watchful. He wondered why the Galactic Empire allowed this warren of shops and hovels to exist here on Glaxius. The very presence of this conclave advertised that the Empire too had its power limits.

Andy had bribed for information at the spaceport hotel; he had his map of the city; and even so the green door he was seeking eluded him at first. He retraced his steps again to search the endless portals, the streets without a name, the houses without a sign, and the innocent appearing green door with no number. When he found the entrance, he knocked with impatience.

"What is it you will have," came the woman's voice from within.

"I wish to trade." It was the true answer, the signal.

"We have little to sell," was the teasing reply. The greatest arms merchant on any of the Free Planets kept up such a front.

"I will buy what you have," he answered.

"What is your name and with what will you buy?"

"I am called Andy Mars. I will use a credit ring." Truth was truth. He had adopted for his last name that of the solar planet he had fled more than a decade ago when his adventure began. He was just one step ahead of the troops of the Empire then. Did everyone hate the Emperor and his Empire? The Empire was all-powerful and now he would fight it and die.

Still there was hesitation inside the green door. The flash in the alleyway where he stood probably indicated sensors and analysis at which he could only guess. The door finally opened, unsealing too quietly, revealing that the entrance was not only protected but also armed.

The woman inside was almost medieval in dress, yet young in years and breathtakingly pretty. She wore a conical hat, a flowing blue dress, incense that filled the room, but in her gray eyes was the narrow searching glint of the trader. She was fragile, with a narrow face, intense appearing, obviously startled by the silver protective uniform of the spacer, and especially by Andy's appearance, the wideness of his shoulders and his great height. She motioned to an oversized purple pillow at the little table opposite her. "Please be seated," she directed.

Andy sat. Perhaps he appeared less threatening that way. "And your name is?" he inquired.

"My name is Sheila Quest." It was an obvious assumed name, as was Andy's. But what was Sheila's quest? "Will you have sadow?" she asked.

"Yes, plain only." The enhancement of the stimulant was fine, but he wanted no mind clouding or consciousness expansion; there was especially no need to reach a mental high and low simultaneously while perhaps going sideways instead. His own drugs might protect him and then again …

The room was ordinary, walls without pictures. Heavy dark green drapes hung behind the slender seated woman, drapes that concealed rooms behind. The plants in the corners were the solitary decorations and some of these were no doubt sensors also. Yes, the room was certainly fully activated, electronically alive, taking his measure.

Andy Mars carried only an ornate dagger as a weapon, and while it was far more than a dagger, yet even this dagger and his protective uniform could not shield him from this room.

His only defense was that he was an unknown quantity, carrying nothing that would make killing him worthwhile.

Sheila Quest nodded, pouring the purple elixir into a glass as might any welcoming hostess. She poured for herself from the same vessel. They toasted. It tasted right. The bracelet on Andy's left wrist glowed blue. He was not being poisoned. Not yet.

"May I view your credit ring?" she requested. If he did not speak the truth, there was hardly a reason to continue the conversation.

Andy Mars held out his left hand. The ring appeared to be of fine gold and contained an inscribed stone that flashed a little even in this artificial light. The credit ring was safe. Its predecessor might have gone back to the beginning of Earthly human traditions, to the Sumerians, over six thousand years ago or 6,000 B.S.A. as they taught them now in school, "Before the Space Age." The wealthy Sumerians wore a ring that had cuneiform carvings that could be pressed upon a clay table as a type of signature, proving who they were, literally sealing transactions. Yet now in spite of progress, in this year 543 ASE, men were still men and women still women. Problems of fraud remained.

Only Andy Mars's ring was more special then the bands of the ancients. When activated it could charge credits against his bank account, guaranteed by the Free Bank, the giant universal credit corporation based on the inner Free Planets.

The credit rings were especially interesting because they were so personal. He could press down the gem upon a parchment agreement and the deductions in credits could be transferred instantly. But if he were killed, the ring would permanently deactivate. If his finger were cut off, which was the only way to remove the ring without his permission, the same thing would occur; the ring would be worthless. Similarly, he could by an effort of will, deactivate the ring. There was no way to steal it or use it for any other purpose than that for which he wished.

Of course he could be threatened, but Andy Mars had long ago decided what to do in difficult situations. He would fight until it was hopeless and then the ring would go. They could kill him, but would receive nothing.

"It is enough. What do you wish to buy?" Sheila inquired.

"I understand you deal in many things. Space craft. Satellites. Even force screens."

Sheila observed the stranger. His smooth skin made the curved scar on his cheek more noticeable. The brown hair showed no gray. He was still young, even after ten years as a star ship navigator. He was also very sure of himself. Sheila decided he was not an Imperial spy, for the court would have chosen someone who did not stand out so much in a crowd. "You are not interested in boxes of blasters for the revolution?" she inquired.

Andy decided that she saw him as toying with her. The blasters would be the major stock in trade for revolutionaries. "It is all contraband," Sheila Quest continued. "What especially are you interested in?"

"Let us start with a force screen."

"You start at the top. You mentioned space craft. A type seven space cruiser with elude," she paused for she saw his eyes narrow. "Yes, with elude, that is twenty billion credits. Are you buying for a confederation in the outer zone?"

She wanted more information than she was giving. "Yes. In a way. A planet in the far outer zone," Andy answered.

"Which planet?"

"Eden."

"Twenty billion credits might exceed the budget of some frontier planets. We need cash in advance."

"You would have the cash. Would such a ship hold a covering force screen?"

"A personal force screen ..."

"No, a ship size force screen, outfitted around a space cruiser with cloaking elude?"

Sheila sat passively a moment. She was calculating. "You are talking in the range of three hundred billion credits."

"And would this invulnerable ship with its force screen, be able to hold and transport the boxes containing a planetary sized force screen component back to my land in one trip?"

Sheila blinked. Her eyes seemed to glaze now. "Do you at all realize what you are talking about? You have not begun to bargain with me, but even so ..." She appeared angry.

The rule of thumb was that you could obtain the goods in the bazaars for half the original quoted amount, but weather that was specifically true here with an arms merchant on quality items of this magnitude was another matter. Andy Mars had done research, but he did not know. Besides he was in a hurry. "Name a figure," he suggested.

The heavy drapes behind Sheila Quest parted. It was obvious the black bearded man in the long purple gown who entered now had been listening all along. He gave no pretense that it might be otherwise. "Stay Sheila," he suggested, gesturing. "My name is Sam. Sam Quest. Sheila is my sister. We are not of this planet." He held both of his hands up next to his face, palms out in the universal gesture of salute. Andy Mars remained seated, but returned the gesture.

The greeting over, Sam Quest sat down on one of the oversize colorful pillows beside Sheila. He had almost savage eyes that he used to good effect now, searching Andy's face. "You have been talking of buying much, and you have flashed your ring, but we do not know if your credit limit is ten or a million. Perhaps you could run a little credit check for us, so we know if we are talking of a blaster or a cruiser or ..." Sam Quest did not finish the sentence.

"Just one more piece of information," Andy Mars requested. "The Empire has planet sized force screens. There are not many planets that even the empire has designated as deserving such a defense, but is it possible to procure a full planetary force screen? Otherwise there is no use running a credit check or anything else. Because while I would like to buy a star cruiser with elude, a planetary force screen is what I am really after. How long would it take to obtain such an item? And what would be your price?"

"That is three questions. The answers are: Yes, we could get one. They are obviously beyond anyone's budget to keep in stock. In fact you must know there are none on planet. It might take twenty standard days. And it might take longer.

The price would be in the neighborhood of eighty trillion credits. I have never had an inquiry on a planetary force shield before, because most wealthy traders stop at covering a city. The military budget of the Galactic Empire was one hundred trillion credits last year. That has been an average budget as the Empire expanded." This last comparison was said with something of a sneer.

"How would this force screen be obtained?"

Sam Quest was angry now. He crossed his arms and sat back in the chair. "Sentinel Industries produces these. They are on the inner free planets, the Citadel Group. They sell them to anyone who will buy. But not directly. There are agents. Even the Empire allows it, because no one but the Empire and the Citadel Group can afford to purchase even one planetary force screen. Why did you not go to Sentinel Industries for your purchase?"

Andy Mars smiled. "I did not go for the reason you have just mentioned. I contacted Sentinel Industries and they gave me a list of agents. You were the first on the list. They do not want to sell such things because they would come under the ban of the Empire. They are already in danger, for the Emperor would like to own their planets too. But if Sentinel Industries sell through agents; they can say they did not know what the use might be."

Sam Quest leaned forward. "All right. There has been much talk. Now, buy something from me, to start our trust in each other, even if it's only a glass of xotil, or get out."

Andy Mars smiled more broadly. "Will you tabulate on your computer your estimated price for a planetary force screen, please."

"Long ago you said one question. You have received much information, and you have given none in return. Who are you really? Is this some form of entrapment? Whom do you represent?"

"I represent the planet Eden and the Chalda Enterprise System. Let us run this credit check."

Sam Quest nodded. His face worked, bunching together. Chalda was known. Everyone bought Chalda. Still, it might be a fraud. But this was interesting. People wanted to feel good, live longer, and stay disease free. The Chalda was bought everywhere and spreading. That was the overpopulation problem now, long life and a healthy old age.

"All right then, let us compute," Sam grunted. Then he looked down at the black flat table between where Andy and Sam were sitting, a table that became a keypad at his touch. He punched out the top figure, before the real bargaining. "Eighty trillion credits. Thirteen lovely zeroes." Sam Quest said aloud, smiling. "This is amusing." Then he sat back and waited.

Andy Mars leaned over the plastic table keypad and pressed his ring down. The corner of the screen glowed green. The full amount was in the Free Bank and guaranteed, available for instant transfer!

Sam Quest turned pale. He felt limp even as his mind buzzed with the possibilities. This was incredible. Even the Emperor, Alexius V, probably could not raise that kind of money without destroying his currency. A wealthy person might have a million credits in a bank. A consortium from a planetary enterprise might have ten million or a hundred million in ready cash, if they were waiting for a major transaction. But this was trillions! Yes, and this was money waiting for a major transaction. It apparently was for real.

Sam Quest had once done a four billion credit deal with the Scandia Alliance just with a credit ring alone. Four years ago in his largest sale, the city-state of Xenia had bought a force screen from him to cover their ten thousand square kilometer base for one trillion credits. It was a deal that Xamia was still paying off in annual installments. This was eighty times larger and all cash. Could it be true? The Free Bank was guaranteeing it. Only there could be no trust on either side with an agreement of this magnitude. No, even a guarantee of the priestesses of Palan would not be sufficient. No group of insurance firms would guarantee it. But the Free Bank said the money was there. It was not just worth pursuing, it was a business deal to retire on and then run and hide in the out worlds before the spies of the Emperor caught up with him. Sam Quest felt his very palms begin to perspire.

He had to issue a warning, a disclaimer to this stranger. Suddenly a great light of understanding seemed to come into Sam Quest's eyes. "I take it, Andy Mars as you call yourself, that the Empire is about to attack Eden and the Emperor Alexius V wishes to take over your Chalda trade? You wish to seal yourself up and resist. I will sell you what you want, but it won't be enough. Nobody defies the Empire successfully."

"Perhaps, but the great game must be played," Andy Mars replied.

The bargaining now began in earnest. "What are your costs?" Andy demanded. "What is your profit margin?"

In an hour they had agreed on 55 trillion, for the ship with elude and its full force screen plus, more importantly, the multi-boxed planetary force screen to be delivered to the ship in twenty days. The installation would be extra. The profit for Sam Quest would be 5 trillion credits, which would allow for transport and bribing the necessary officials. Then Sam Quest would leave for the Far Out, and set up on his own world. Five trillion profit! He would not admit to such a profit even if cornered.

But the details remained. "The credits will be transferred to your account only when I am back on Eden with the force screen," Andy Mars demanded. "The full amount of the money will be encumbered, but placed on hold until then."

Sam Quest began to ruminate upon other matters: "The Empire had to allow the Citadel Group to force screen themselves," he declared. "But there are those on some planets who have thought to safeguard cities with force screens, and some of those cities have seen what happened afterwards when they crossed the Emperor in their pride. Armed forces landed and burrowed beneath the screened city and blew it, screen and all. The Emperor will not take kindly to anyone closing themselves off completely on their entire planet. Do you know what you are doing? If a planet bought a force screen and were in no danger to the Empire and had nothing Emperor Alexius

V wanted, they might get away with this. But you have something everyone wants, the Chalda Plant and its elixir. So the Imperial troops will come. And they are persistent. You may well be able to have time to get this planetary force screen installed, but its purpose will be known."

"Force shields are purely defensive," Andy Mars declared smiling. "That is the nature of force screens."

"True. But it will be like a beacon to the Galactic Empire, a challenge hurled down. I can not sell you this without warning you. I personally will take my profit and run."

"Understood. There will be major trouble. But I am about to have trouble in the form of an invasion in any case. I am preparing for interplanetary war. Of course the free cities that manufacture the screens are allowed to be secure. They have installed their own planetary force screens. They have nothing else the Emperor wants for now." Andy Mars smiled again. "I have seen trouble before. There is one other thing. I would ask that you and your sister Sheila come with me to Eden to stay until the goods are delivered."

Sam nodded. There was so much at stake. Could he make this work for this crazy rich man? And Sam knew he would have to make sure Andy Mars did not keep them both prisoners, beyond the possibility of escape, with a planetary force screen. Once the wrath of the Empire descended upon them, Sam and his sister had both better be long gone.

"Am I chattel to be shipped off as part of this agreement?" Sheila Quest asked. She knew what was involved, but yet felt the need to protest.

"You and Sam both may stay on Eden as long as you wish," Andy countered. "Sheila, you are a beautiful woman, and certainly not chattel in any sense. Because of the Pilgrim religion and what has happened with the Chalda, I am already married to three women, only one of whom I love. But that is another story. When the force screen is installed, you and Sam may build a palace with your profits and force screen it within the planetary screen on Eden, or leave as pleases you. You have my word on it. It is a word backed by the

Chalda and the Plant God whom you will meet. There is presently much virgin land on Eden.

The economic power of the Chalda drug was well known to Sam Quest. Sam laughed. "That way you will have us there till the job is completed. You do realize how much power a planetary force screen will use when it is in place? Do you have the nuclear capacity to run this? Whatever power for cities or industry you utilize now on your planet, this force screen will quadruple your needs."

"We are ready for that."

Sam Quest nodded. "You do also realize that Planetary Force Screens may be sabotaged from the inside. Spies of the Emperor are in place on virgin planets everywhere. The Emperor does not go after Mother Earth yet because he wants everything else first. Mother Earth has force screens everywhere, but it is crowded and not particularly valuable because of the overpopulation. I must tell you these things honestly. Force screens have never been tested in battle. You will get what you pay for, but there can be no guarantees. The Empire has many scientists and countermeasures will be found."

Andy also nodded. "I understand what you say."

Sam Quest reflected one last time. The deal was too lucrative to turn down even with the dangers. It was a sale to give your life to, and that might be the case.

So Andy Mars and Sam Quest entered upon the heart of the high adventure that had begun with the Planet Eden and the Chalda Thorn.

2

EDEN

It was several years now since Andy Mars entered into what he called his third life, that of a farmer on Eden, the water planet, the Plant Planet some called it, with all its deadly mysteries, the home of the Plant God. The Pilgrims named it Eden because it seemed to be a land of eternal spring. Here the strange series of events began with so many wild results. And here was set into motion the occurrences that finally resulted in interplanetary war with the Empire and the final defeat.

It was after the sting, when the Chalda Thorn, half a meter long, struck his back and began to disgorge its poison. At that time Andy Mars knew he was dying. He had attempted to pull away and only partly succeeded. Then he started back to Myra and his house on the hill, slowing down at once as the strength drained from him. There was so much life to live yet. He even tried the techniques he had mastered at the Golden Pavilion, the Great Monastery of Peace where he had studied on the world called Sanctuary. He attempted to use the knowledge learned at Sanctuary to remove his body from the poison of the sting, to isolate the venom, but it was too late to stop most of the spreading death. It was so stupid to die this way. To be killed by a weed. Well, he had been fully warned many times!

It was then that the first of the strange events took place. He stumbled and leaned against a huge gnarled vine, one of the tangled aboveground roots of the forest that traveled for hundreds of kilometers over hills and valleys. The root was a thick round herbage, well over two meters in diameter, Andy's own height, big as a space freighter barrel and as long as the wind.

Andy Mars leaned against the dark brown bark of this enormous vine, gasping for breath already, sweating profusely with the beginning of the death. In back of him was all the greenery of the cleared land, stretching out as it sloped upward to the House on the hill. In front of him, beyond the huge round aboveground root was the profusion of jungle that went for kilometers, thick, unrelenting. Here Andy had cautiously ventured, cutting at vines with a blaster. Then, as he so carefully stepped into the jungle, had the Chalda Thorn struck at him. The wines must be set almost as a hair-trigger, a spring action of one vine supporting another under tension, until the plant was jostled and then the thorn could strike like a dagger. Now Andy was afraid to lie down or do more than cling to the folds of the giant twisted root, for he might not be able to ever arise again.

Then he felt the words, the thought. It came on slowly, with all the time on the planet to form: "Which of us is the weed Andy Mars?"

It was not his own thought; it had to come from outside. It was a concept without meaning to him at first. Andy turned his head to look around and then spoke an answer aloud to no one in particular: "Who sends ideas to me now?" Perhaps this was death calling, as the Pilgrims here believed would happen.

The words formed again, softly as the high grass blows in the breeze: "You are relaxed against my receptor. Your roots, what you call your veins, are coursing with a deadly plant elixir stronger than you are. It actually helps us to communicate. Still it is a purposeful contaminant that infects you and it may kill you."

"Are you connected to the Chalda Thorn that has struck me?" Andy asked weakly, but aloud.

"No. We are separate. The Chalda Thorn does not communicate."

"You are the network root that spreads and wanders everywhere on this land?" Andy Mars questioned, speaking aloud. "No, matter, the Chalda Thorn has scratched me, and I shall die." He laughed savagely.

"You may die. You are gravely injured. But my question remains unanswered: I see the word 'weed,' used for many plants in your mind. Which of us is the interloper? You are a stranger, not originally of this planet. Yet you are filled with hate just now, because you have been poisoned. But which should die? For I too can kill, though I am not indiscriminate as the Chalda Thorn?"

Andy Mars thought. Plant philosophy at the end of his life. Again he spoke aloud: "I guess I am too indiscriminate. It is a true challenge you suggest to me. I kill plants that get in the way of my producing food for my family. I leave the native grass and the plants I consider pretty." This plant root suggested he might not die. Life was indeed sweet. He would humble himself before a blade of grass, if it meant he could survive.

"What is beauty, Andy Mars?"

He would have laughed in other circumstances. "That too is a question for the philosophers. If I live, we will discuss this further. I am worried about dying now. Is there anything you can suggest that will help me?"

"Is a weed merely a plant out of place within the realm of human control?" The thoughts again entered his mind, clearer than spoken words. "Is a weed only a plant for which you have not yet found a use? Do men finding a use determine what plants survive to serve him?"

"Perhaps," Andy replied. "I am not wise enough to know." He was feeling desperate right now and very vulnerable. It was a new experience indeed. Always he had been so sure of himself; now suddenly he was certain of nothing. It seemed to Andy that the plant was testing him and might only help if his answers pleased. He felt the sweat of death upon his body.

The words came on, thick as seeds in the forest: "There is a harmony in nature, Andy Mars. There is a balance. There is a unity to the universe. There is a brotherhood of all life. Life is the measure of all things, not man alone. Life is related. Are plants to be judged by their use to man? Without plants, there could be no animals. Do you understand that? Plants can exist without animals. Animals can not exist without plants. Plants are therefore primary. Yes, animals may eat each other, but at the bottom of the animal food chain there must be plants to begin it all. You are a part of life, not separate to judge."

"Before I came here to this planet, fleeing, I was many things in my first life," Andy Mars replied, speaking aloud, not knowing which way to even direct his words. Nor did he care. The communication was there. And it was high level talk. It was intriguing, even if these were his last words. "Now I am a farmer on this planet. I use my knowledge of chemistry and biology to grow plants and try to survive. You wish me to live as one with the plants. Yet I have never spoken to plants before. I will tell you honestly that on Earth, where I come from, it rains on man's schedule almost every night over the whole planet. Humans have altered the weather patterns. Humans decide which plants they will farm and which will receive water. Perhaps water is primary. And the humans decide." Now perhaps he had offended this plant and would pay with his life.

It was one thing to communicate telepathically with a plant, but this plant's clever use of the universal galactic language of humans seemed to be quite another matter to Andy. It was best to change the subject. "You have been listening to humans talk," Andy declared.

"Yes, in the capital city, far down the river, the town that is called Lorraine. My roots are used as bridges across the river there. The people talk as they cross the river."

"But you have not attempted to converse with any of these people?" Andy inquired.

"No. I am too exposed in the town. Here we are alone."

"And you have me at your disposal," Andy suggested.

"Yes, that is true. It is private here at the edge of the forest. We are alone. I like that."

Andy felt the flush of fever and the rash beginning to cover his body. He was sure he could not even make it back to the house on the hill to die. They would find his body here at the edge of the clearing, only a kilometer from his home, as with so many of the others who had gone out into the jungle and never returned alive.

*   *   *

"I'm not afraid of the Chalda Thorn," Andy Mars had told Myra, just days before. "I respect it. I am careful."

And Myra, his best wife, the most beautiful woman he had ever known, she had replied: "The Chalda has killed so many on this planet. Why do you feel invulnerable?"

"We are here. This is a water planet. It is beautiful land, perfect in its tropical climate, lush with greenery, and yet the land area on this entire planet is so small that this world has been bypassed by most in the tremendous human migration."

Myra rubbed her high cheeks and purred. "I love you partly because you are a dreamer, Andy Mars. Eden, as the Pilgrims call this place, has not been bypassed; it is so far out, it is scarcely known. Eden is beautiful, but deadly. Last week alone three of the men in just this village died of the Chalda Thorn. Were they not careful? Did they seek out death and embrace it? The Pilgrims say it is God's will when someone dies. One of those men who died was your friend, David Larx. Did he not study biology too? If we are going to live on the edge of the explored worlds in this galaxy, on the very fringe of the space frontiers, let us go even yet further into the deep unknown and find a world without such problems."

But Andy Mars had run away long enough. "We will stay on Eden," he determined. "There is nothing in this life without problems. There are only kinds of problems and many types of solutions. We have even made peace with the Pilgrims and we will embrace their religion if need be. And I shall be careful."

Myra was left alone and had plenty of time for thinking. If Andy ever really knew about her, her terrible secret, what would he do? Andy had been born on Earth. He had studied on Mars and then run from Mars and was an outlaw in the eyes of the Empire.

Once, several years ago now, in one of Myra's classes, a Professor had declared that the relationship of men and women went back to Earth's early tribal societies, a million years ago, thousands of generations. During this long period men went off and hunted, fought, and explored, while women stayed in the camp. The ideal of the good wife was one who stayed put and obeyed orders. Women were more likely to remain in place than men. If they didn't stay put, they often didn't have children or the children died, because the women were the chief protectors of the children.

That explained men and their desire that women be pure and never have looked at another man. Myra reflected in amusement that women were just supposed to have hung themselves on a hook in a closet waiting for the right man. They must be forever true. She loved Andy Mars, but she had looked at other men.

If that wasn't normal, then she wasn't normal. But her secret was far worse than a furtive glance, or even relations with other men.

When Happy and Felicity were pushed upon Andy as new wives, it was the Pilgrim "Village Elders" who were forcing him to adopt their new way of life. It was planned promiscuity. Myra had accepted the lesser wives because of her own enormous guilty secret.

On Eden hundreds had died of the Chalda Thorn, largely men. More were dying every week. Whatever the problem was, just recognizing the triangular leaf of the poisonous Chalda Thorn was not enough. Saying it was God's will was not sufficient for Myra. She believed that this planet, so perfect in climate and oxygen, was not created by God but cursed by the Devil!

The Pilgrims had spent their money getting here and now they were in a trap. They had no choice now but to farm. But farming was what they wanted anyway.

Many of the original settlers who came before the Pilgrims arrived had led very rough and tumble lives in and around their little capital settlement at Lorraine. The Pilgrims had branched out moving upriver. They were willing to work hard. Wanting their own community, they had moved off into the forests and jungles to farm. They had even succeeded in having the planet renamed Eden.

Especially the Pilgrims seemed dedicated to building homes and establishing communities, farming and raising sheep as the original Christians. They had imported the embryos of the sheep with them on the long journey from Earth. The Pilgrims wanted to be shepherds in the ancient Biblical sense. The sheep were fenced in on cleared land so they did not drift off to be killed by the Chalda Thorn. Even the range chickens, contained by an invisible electronic fence, were secured from the Chalda death. But the men went out into new lands to clear the thick forests. They tried to farm and died.

The Pilgrims cut down trees to build homes. The pattern was clear. Farmers farmed. They ventured forth clearing the virgin land on this planet and they died when the Chalda Thorn struck them down. The Bishops and Prophets, who were the Pilgrim leaders, stayed behind in the new village and were safe. The widowed wives were divided up among the remaining men. Andy was asked to take additional wives. Myra felt the elders of the church, who had all taken more wives, would be accused of lewd living, if Andy and others in the flock did not participate. Besides the Pilgrims wished to increase their population. Only Andy wanted to master his land before he had children. So the unfulfilled women waited for him, wives without children.

Myra knew that when Andy died of the Chalda Thorn the Pilgrim Elders would try to force her on someone else. Then she would hitch a ride to the next planet. Her money was nearly gone and things looked bleak. She lay awake nights beside Andy, such a huge man and so clever with plants, and now he would die of the Chalda Thorn. When you feel trapped and there is no way out, your mind keeps going around and around. All the escapes from this planet were without Andy and she did not want that.

* * *

"Is there a secret? Is there a way to survive the Chalda?" Andy Mars was leaning against the Great Root that traveled across the valley for kilometers and forded the very streams to continue endlessly beyond. And he was talking aloud to a plant. It seemed so absurd. Yet the communication was there. Or was he in a delirium of head throbbing death already, dreaming all of this? His body was filled with the buzzing of a growing fever.

The words of reply drifted back to enter his consciousness: "'Symbiosis,' you call it. An agreement between creatures to help each other. Are you willing to help me, when I call in my debt?"

"Yes." Andy Mars felt the first of the involuntary shakes. He was beginning to twitch all over. "Andy, most ambulatory creatures are stung much more severely by the Chalda Thorn and die at once," came the thought hammering into his head now. "Further, you are strong for your species. You might survive anyway. Beyond that, my help is minimal yet it may be enough at close calls. Do you still accept my terms?"

"Yes." He accepted without even knowing what he might be asked. The drowning man clings to the smallest twig.

"You will return right here if you recover."

"Agreed."

"Remove your shirt and make further contact with my surface."

Obeying a plant. It was good to remove his heavy shirt which was soaked with sweat now. He tottered and could barely remain standing. Contact. What did it mean? Andy spread out, placing his naked arms and hairy chest upon the huge root. Waiting. Nothing seemed to happen.

Almost he laughed. A madness of mirth before death. Then he felt an inner peace come over him. He was calmer, more relaxed. The shakes left him.

There was a silly old human phrase, "Hunger for wholeness," drifting into his thoughts. Words from a plant taken from his mind, perhaps.

Yes, he was better. Before death had seemed certain, now he believed he actually had a chance. The Pilgrims talked of their meetings as "Communion," and the word came into his mind. Communion. Contact. "Thank you," he whispered. "If I live, I will certainly return."

He left the perspiration soaked shirt lying on the ground in this place of mystery, a flag perhaps, a cynosure, so he would know precisely where he was now, if he ever came back alive. Then he struck out in shaky fashion for the clearing and the house on the hill where Myra and the other wives waited.

*   *   *

Myra went pale when she saw Andy Mars tottering along the path and ran out to help him, calling to the lesser wives for assistance. For three days he hovered between life and death, feverish, shaking at times, sleeping most of the over long days.

Myra used the last of her makeup so she would not look pale and show Andy how frightened she was. She turned her head away to cry on that first day. The Pilgrim women used no artifices nor could you buy makeup here in this backcountry village.

Yet to Myra it was almost a good time, once she saw Andy would recover, for he was so weak, so completely dependent. She attended to him personally. She had naturally installed him in her room until his illness was over. She ordered Felicity and Happy about on the chores and spent all of her time attending Andy. She realized again how much she loved him. The horrible thought came: how pleasant it would be if Andy just continued like this, lying here completely at her whim. She banished that thought and looked at his pale form, the telltale rash of the Chalda, the sweating and fever. The other wives came in obediently with trays of food for Myra and a little broth for Andy.

Felicity and Happy were true Pilgrims, with their forever-uncut straight long brown hair and wide, unadorned faces. They both had the broad continence of the Pilgrim: intermarriage had produced a similarity. But even Pilgrims varied.

Happy was accident-prone, and could start from the kitchen, where she cut herself, to the bathroom for medication, where she would drop something, to the communication room, where she habitually ran into the table corner with her leg. Andy would ask her where she had bruised herself today, and she would show him her latest injuries, laughing liltingly at herself. "It is the Lord's will," she declared once. "I am being punished."

"Don't blame the Lord because you are a flake," Andy retorted.

Happy had been competitive with the other wife when her second husband had two wives. She attempted to entice him, tried for a larger share of the time of the new man. Now with Andy she had given up. She allowed Andy to decide. It was probably all her fault her husbands had died. She had been filled with sinful thoughts, pride, and lust.

Happy told Andy she hoped there would not be a fourth wife. She also suggested to Andy that she wished he would not farm, but open a shop in the village, and therefore not die of the Chalda Thorn. She had been married twice before and widowed both times. The changes in her life she saw as preordained and she had become very philosophical. Whatever will be will be was her new motto, and she felt her religion demanded she accept life as it came. She was jinxed. She cried over her first husband's death for many nights, which angered the second. She now felt Andy was the best of all, but he too farmed, clearing the jungle land. He too would die.

*　　*　　*

Both Happy and Felicity tried to cheer Myra, now that Andy had been struck down. Felicity suggested that since Andy had not died instantly, and was so big, that God was showing him mercy. They loved him too, in their own way. Give your child a name like Felicity or Happy and they often tried to fit the appellation. Some cases in point were the Pilgrim woman in the village named Bountiful, who had fourteen children or Harmony, a wife of Good Bishop Swife, who visited the farmers and smoothed over so many family difficulties. But there were other Pilgrims where the name did not fit.

Myra was always the most passionate of Andy's wives. During their lovemaking, when he slept with her, she turned the room music way up, to cover all the noise she made. Once, when Andy commented, amused at her outcry, Myra declared: "It relieves my tensions to scream and call out, and I feel better. It heightens every sensation. I feel better at the time of lovemaking and afterwards as well. Your Pilgrim girls believe they must conceal all emotion, or isn't that true?"

It was true, but Andy would not talk about the others. The Pilgrim women had been taught submission to the man as divinely ordained. Andy would not mention that Happy hummed a little tune after making love or that Felicity fell asleep with a most contented smile. The first time he had made love with Felicity she scared him. In climax she suddenly tensed up, shook her head, and her eyes literally rolled back in their sockets so that Andy could only see the whites. Then she fell asleep and began breathing normally again.

When Andy and Myra had first agreed to convert and become one with the Pilgrims, neither had realized that it would mean he must take on other wives. Myra did not complain at all, for this seemed a fitting punishment to her; quite right when she considered her childhood and the dangerous mysteries she had withheld from Andy. Myra told Andy once, when they were alone in their room: "The ways of Earth have become strange. All the original cultures have broken down due to overpopulation. At one point, in 300 A.S.A., there were too few women on Earth and now there are too many women here on Eden. It changes culture. The original Christians would not have accepted this state of affairs on Earth or on Eden."

Andy agreed, but said simply: "You are my favorite and in charge. I have made that clear. You are the one I came to Eden with. We began alone on the splendid space station resort on Belleine: I feel our love can never change. But unless we go off alone in the wilds to the far stars, we can't escape the conditions of living with other people."

Andy thought of all this. The Pilgrims called this Eden, because it was to be the new Paradise. They lived apart from the other people on this planet, away from the small towns. They had established their own small village along a wide river, which they named Jordan. Gradually the Pilgrim name for the planet, Eden, had been accepted by the other people of the new world. The Pilgrims began to farm and sent men out exploring, and the explorers died by the dozen of the Chalda Thorn. It was the snake in the Garden of Eden they said, and would only strike the unholy.

At first the loss of life among the Pilgrims had been appalling. So many died and their bodies were just found at the edge of the clearings where they had been attacking the persistent jungle. They never made it home from the Chalda sting to explain what had killed them. Many felt in this time of uncertainty that it was the Lord's Will. The wicked were being slain. Only gradually was the triangular leaf identified, the delta warning of the Chalda discovered and the thorn blamed and avoided. But still, what was not seen in taming the jungle was that the Chalda Thorn had its own way.

Andy Mars had now discovered there was a tension to the Chalda vine that created a spring like trap, sending the thorn of death into anyone who came close.

Andy Mars' two added wives were a gift of his conversion, a dual set as if to show there was no carnality intended on his part. There was an attempt at balance. Some of the elders of the church had four wives; most of the congregation had three.

Happy and Felicity knew that Andy Mars had been an outsider, coming here with Myra, seeking refuge, a place to live. An extensive farm was possible on Eden, a planet off the main traveled space routes. It was far from the Empire and not even associated with the loose league of independent Free Planets. The Pilgrims accepted Andy, his semi-conversion to their ways, his willingness to abide by their ancient laws, and his agreement to call the planet Eden. And Eden seemed a fitting name for a fertile, green, lush planet, a world of tropical and rather constant temperature, heavy in oxygen, redolent, a fragrance that soothed the human psyche.

Before he had gone to the University on Mars, Andy had traveled about on Mother Earth, visiting the Holy Lands there that had now come under the World Federation's control to finally bring peace to the troubled region. This was all centuries after the Terrorist Nuclear Wars on earth. Since then the force screens finally brought peace. When Andy visited the warm Holy Lands on Earth, he could not conceive that the paintings of the early Christians amid Christmas snow could be correct. Perhaps things had changed over the centuries. So too tropical planet Eden was devoid of snow. Here were mysteries.

Andy Mars looked back on his chance meeting with Myra Deets as the most important day in his life. At first he had thought perhaps she was an Imperial spy, but Andy was hardly worth keeping tabs on at that time. Still when he saw her travel pass he knew it had been cleverly altered. Andy slowly came to realize that there was some great secret about Myra he was not supposed to inquire into yet.

They had met in a spaceport lounge, with Andy flush from his successful training on the world of Sanctuary.

The Mystic One had even predicted he would soon find the right woman and path for his life. The Predictor had it correct as usual and Eden seemed to be the place to settle. Myra had said later that it was best if people were introduced somehow, as in the old tradition.

But their meeting had been anything but the old traditions. Myra had been seated across the hundred meter long oval bar from Andy. She smiled at him, a radiant searchlight smile. She was a diminutive creature, but an obvious mammal with a beautiful full face. Andy was not sure he even wanted to get involved, and he sat immobile for a bit, smiling back tentatively. Then she winked.

Andy arose uncertainly and brought his drink over. He had no pick-up line; indeed any statement he made might lead to a retreat. The closer he got the prettier she looked. She kept the docking lights of her incendiary smile lit all the way in to port.

"You called?" he asked.

"Yes," she answered, laughing a tinkling of merriment. "The rules, you know," Myra added.

"And what are these rules?"

"The woman sits back and the man comes to her."

"And if he does not come?"

"Then you help him realize what he must do."

"So are there any lines you haven't heard?"

"It's not the line or the bait, but is there any substance."

"My name is Andy Mars."

"And I am Myra Deets. I have had a sheltered life, so I am practicing how to flirt."

"Does it work?"

"Oh yes. It is like fishing we were talking about. You sit and throw out a line and wait."

"And are all the fish equally pleasing?"

"No." Again there was the tinkling little laugh, not at Andy but at herself.

"If you get the wrong fish?" Andy asked. He was still standing beside her, thinking.

"You throw it back."

"How are my scales?"

"I am still weighing."

Now Andy laughed and sat down. "May I buy you a drink?"

"I thought you'd never ask," Myra answered.

Andy wondered later why the minutest details of the fresh love were so important. Sure, for centuries scientists had studied the brain receptors for dopamine, causing all with a new love to experience dopery indeed.

After that meeting Andy had first taken Myra to the enormous spaceport resort on Belleine. He remembered what he always thought of as the "splendid day." It was a whole standard day of lying in bed and making love, kissing, talking, long silences, interspersed by short bursts of questions and answers while looking at each other. Andy thought later that if this day could pass, all of life could. There was no holding anything in the tight fist of time. Life was all too illusive, too transitory, a meaningless shifting shadow, tricking you that it was real, and each sliced moment here alone with Myra was perfect rapture.

Now on Eden, would it be desertion to leave two wives flat and run off with Myra his original wife? It was why he avoided having children with any of them. The trap of children sprang on people and then you must take the whole clan, the relatives, the in-laws and the outlaws. The responsibility was there. He did not know what he wanted to do with the rest of his life yet.

Myra had time to think as Andy slept after the Chalda Thorn sting. She had been aware of the effect of bonding with a man. Every day she was with Andy she loved him more, adapted to his ways more. Perhaps now he would leave this planet of death with her alone. What could ever be done to resolve this situation otherwise? What would Andy think if he knew the real truth about her background? Then Andy awoke, hungry on the fourth day, feeling better. And now the peculiar thing began.

In a week Andy Mars felt better than he ever had. He not only regained his former enormous strength, but he felt more alive than before. The feeling was too obviously something so completely new it could not be dismissed. It was a time before he realized the full scope, the enormous importance of what this new feeling meant.

*　*　*

True to his word, Andy Mars returned to the wide clearing in the valley where the Great Root crossed the open grasslands. Here for just a bit, before it returned to the forest to run along for kilometers until it was out of sight again, the root was in the open, exposed. Andy examined the Root closely. He could see that smaller vines of the Great Root branched off in places to sink into the ground while in other areas spiraling trees with huge leaves were growing from the root, every hundred meters or so. The trees of this root were giants, climbing over a hundred meters skyward and were the tallest plants in the jungle.

In the confusion of this wilderness, there was symmetry to this particular plant, hidden by the tangled growth of the other vegetation. Only gradually did Andy Mars see the root was using the jungle as its own protective screen, a way to hide its enormous extent.

Andy Mars stood next to the root for a long time. No words entering his mind. Was it delirium? Had he dreamt the whole conversation? Was the great plant asleep? Andy was alive and it was enough. His gaze followed the gnarled root running off down the hill and up, lost in the greenery of thousands of plants growing over and above it. But always the root emerged to continue to the crest of the next hill and down across the stream below.

He saw his shirt where he had left it, and stooped to pick it up. Then the words came into his consciousness at last: "Move to your right, please."

Andy felt the faintness of the words and wondered. He walked a few meters down a slope in the clearing and stood before the Great Root. Perhaps he had been in the wrong place.

"It is good that you recovered. It is good you returned. You are a man of honor. Tell me about humans. Begin with yourself."

Andy tried to analyze how the words were transmitted so sharply into his brain.

"Your trees are beautiful," he declared. It was the best of flattery, for he meant it. "I hope the townspeople and Pilgrims have not cut down any trees belonging to you."

"Yes, they have. But they did not know. And it does not matter as long as they do not attack my major roots. I just terminated sensory perception with the tree being cut. I do not possess a sense of pain anyway. But it is a matter I wish to discuss with you."

There was a pause and then the Great Root thoughts continued: "Andy, a woman sat on one of my root bridges, the one over the river near the city of Lorraine, where I have deliberately run three roots across connected with vines. I raised these roots from the river bottom where they were out of sight and made a bridge. Anyway this woman sat waiting for someone. I felt her presence and form. She was clipping her fingernails." The Great Root paused.

"Yes?" Andy asked uncertainly. The Great Root could not see her. How did the Great Root know what she was doing? Andy was back to evil black thoughts. Could the Great Root read minds after all? Maybe the Root could read only what was at the forefront of human consciousness. Or … Andy's thoughts were interrupted.

"Does clipping fingernails or cutting hair hurt?" the Great Root inquired.

"No," Andy laughed.

"I thought not. Well it is the same when I withdraw myself from a plant whose flowers are cut or a tree that is cut. And there is more."

"Yes?"

"I believe my not feeling pain is an advantage. I have no pain receptors. I feel fire caused by lightning strikes, though the abundant rain here, on what you call Eden, precludes many fires. I have felt a fire destroying parts of "me" but pain sensations would not be useful to me. I can not withdraw a hand or foot. In my early days when some other plants sought to strangle my roots, I felt no pain, only pressure which I resisted."

"So how did you deal with attack from other plants?"

"I learned to subsume some plants that were dangerous to me. But long ago I decided on a policy of diversity. Other plants could live, but I simply pushed them back if they attacked me."

"I suppose humans and animals have a sense of pain because it is evolutionarily useful. They jump when bitten, burned, or cut. Plants can not move that fast. They grow slowly."

"Plants do move slowly, but they can avoid objects in their way and even attack."

"Attack how?"

"The small roots of nearby plants are always in competition for soil and water. They may even strangle each other to spread and live."

"So what do you mean by subsume?"

"To move tightly, twisting around another root and invade it until it becomes part of me." Andy saw the process as akin to grafting, one plant becoming another.

"And humans, are they a danger to you?"

"That is why we are having this conversation, Andy. As yet I have not struck back against humans, but if they attack my roots, there will be trouble."

"What will you do?"

"First converse, as we are doing, then warn. Finally, well the Pilgrims raise sheep that eat the grass that could become poisoned. The humans eat vegetables from their gardens that could become harmful. I am more of the plant life than you realize."

Andy was appalled at the threat. "Your wood may be the best, since it has to be very hard wood to grow so tall," he answered at last. And you are not the Chalda."

"No. I do not kill indiscriminately for no reason. I have purposely avoided becoming all the plants on the planet to continue the diversity of life. I can live together with humans. Describe human evolution for me Andy?"

Andy was analytical: "Lesser creatures, false starts, divergence, chance, and finally man. In the last century men have spread out and changed more extensively than ever before, looking back on millions of years of human transitions."

The Great Root wanted further information, asking about the other animals on Earth. "I need to bring books to read to you," Andy finally declared. "How," he asked, "did you attain consciousness, a sense of self?"

"Solitary evolution. I do not know. It just happened. Slowly I possessed thought and struggled for more. Perhaps it was a part of my great growth everywhere on this planet."

There was a piece of the puzzle missing here, Andy decided, something the Great Root was not telling. "Men learned speech by talking to each other. How does an isolated intelligence learn this?" Andy asked.

"You are right. I spoke first to the river lizards, not in words but in pure thought as I am doing with you. For centuries I lived in darkness and thought I was alone. It was the river lizards who first communicated to me, telepathically. We will talk on that later."

And then again the Root switched the subject from itself to Andy and humans: "You spoke of my trees, Andy. Humans have a sense of possessing the plants, the animals, the land. I feel it can lead to trouble for them."

"Yes. Long ago when new settlers came to a place called America on Earth, the native populations were primitive and had little sense of possessing the land. Soon, without meaning to, the original inhabitants, called Indians, had signed away the rights to their land to the newcomers. As to your trees, if you caused them to grow along a human road in a straight line, and sent up your hundred meter high trees symmetrically, it would have a very pleasing effect for humans."

"You see things in human terms. I have tolerated the other plants because they too deserve to live. Lately the other plants have also obscured my presence from humans. Is beauty only in the eye of humans Andy? Some plants produce perfume to attract insects to spread their seeds. Humans think the perfume is for them. That is egocentric. So tell me about your life, Andy Mars."

It was necessary to reply. "Farming on Eden was not what I thought my life would be," Andy Mars began simply. Since the words from the Root entered his mind as thoughts, unspoken, yet vivid, it might be the Root could read his very mind. But to what extent?

Andy asked: "When I first came into contact with you, I believed I would die. Nothing that I thought or said really mattered. Now that I have found I will live, I would like to inquire: Can you read my mind?" Would the plant tell the truth, if it wanted to cover up its abilities?

"No. I can read your thoughts, even if you do not express them, in what you call speech. But these must be major thoughts, you are really concentrating on. I would not ask questions, if I could see into all of your memories and pluck forth everything from what you call your mind. When we first came into contact, you had been struck by the Chalda Thorn, and were angry, thinking that you wished you could destroy all such weeds. That prompted my question about which of us was the weed. Now that I know you better, I feel you are superior to the Chalda."

That was progress. "Thank you," Andy replied. Possibly the questions were needed to make him think of the information the Root wished to extract. Would the Root turn upon him in some way if he showed fear or anger?

And Andy Mars related his life story aloud in as simple a fashion as he could. Each Pilgrim farmer believed in his own safety from the

Chalda because God would protect him. Andy Mars' protection had been his studies of plants as a biologist and examining the strange alien life forms of many planets. But his knowledge of plants had not been enough.

He told the Root about his life on Earth and Mars. He described the University on Mars with its suburb laboratories, the enormous vaulting towers where he had studied as a young man. He never joined the secret rebels who protested against the Empire. He never did more than study and go out with a few friends. But still the disaster happened. He explained his early life to the Great Root, trying not to make humans look bad, but he could not conceal his present hatred of the Galactic Empire.

There have always been empires on Earth, the Assyrian, the Persian, the Egyptian, the Roman, and the Mongol, to name a few, in the deep past. Now there was an Empire in the stars. The Galactic Empire held forty-six suns and their planets under its iron fist. Forty-six and spreading out.

Any move by the free planets to unite brought instant attack upon the centers of a conspiracy. Most of the free planets were jealous of each other, proud of their independence, hoping to just continue without arousing the Imperial forces. The Imperial spies were everywhere. And the huge human migration was continuing to further outworlds.

From adulthood on Andy Mars was always so big, such a giant of a man, that others regarded him as a sports person, but he never had time. Nor did he participate in the air skiing that led to the death of one of his best friends at the university.

Andy was one of those selected on graduation for the Mars Academy; the splendid towered graduate school on Mars where so many of the specimens of alien life forms from the stars were brought back to be studied. As a biologist he found it odd to be studying plants in thousands of greenhouses on Mars, a cold planet with a thin atmosphere. Mars had been terraformed and was livable, but most people stayed inside the terraced buildings. Still it was good to escape from the Earth, the enormous crowds of people, the beehive cities, and even the computerized farms where he spent his childhood.

His favorite professor had told the class that as graduate students they had mastered the books and computers. But now it was to nature they must turn, to see what life was really all about. "Do not trust the books and computers too much, but see for yourself." The professor quoted 19th century Louis Agassiz, "The book of nature is always open." Even then, working in the greenhouse among the plants Andy, felt a communication, as if these living things and he were one. He felt love and reverence for the greenery.

At the University Andy realized he was too much the loner, too immersed in his studies. The University on Mars was funded by and sponsored by the Empire, to show the nearby Earth that the Empire was good. The Empire had never touched Mother Earth. Of course the overpopulated Earth with all of its continuing problems was not worth much to the Empire.

When the group of nine rebel University students was caught and tortured, they confessed to the treason against the Empire. It was demanded they give the names of all the conspirators. At first the rebels declared no others had distributed the publications, which was possibly true. Then as the torturing pain became more severe, others were named, and any name would do. It was akin to those in the Medieval Inquisitions in the long ago time on Earth, those who were tied to the rack and asked if they were in league with the Devil, until they finally confessed to anything and then they were burned at the stake. Someone had named Andy Mars, and he had fled. Two Imperial Guards had come for him and Andy had simply smashed them both.

He took refuge on an outworld ship and soon became a spacer with many names and cargoes. He let go of his original name, and became simply Andy Mars, after the planet he had been forced to flee. Soon he had false papers that made him out a navigator of the void, and he bluffed his way onto huge star ships, first freighters and later passenger liners. He learned and studied all about these ships.

But his interest in biology had remained in the back of his mind, waiting. His first life was that of the university and his second life that of the space master. Now in his third life he was a farmer on Eden.

Andy Mars paused in his tale; his story he was telling the Great Root and the question came into his mind from the Root. "Earth was the original planet of humans?"

"Yes."

"Tell me about it."

"The population control was fierce. What will happen, Great Root, when you are everywhere on this planet, Eden? Is there a limit?"

"I already limit myself," the Root responded. "Since I am alone, that is fairly easy. So tell me about the Earth's population control."

"There was a tilt toward genetic superiority. Only those who were physically fit and very intelligent, those with a University Degree, with special achievements, were allowed to have up to three children. All others were allowed one or two, depending upon whim of category. Defective humans were not allowed any children, and the definitions of defective varied. To violate that rule meant death for the parents and all their children. The real problem for men was to find a wife."

"It was an amusing dilemma," Andy Mars continued, now somehow accustomed to talking to wood, speaking aloud to a plant being, an entity without a mouth or vocal cords, who replied only telepathically. "Once a long time ago on Earth women had been downgraded in some cultures. When populations grew due to better health and medicine, rigid population control was tried. There were phases of change. For a time people were allowed to have only one child. As soon as people could decide on the sex of their children, many more humans chose to have male offspring. Since they were only allowed one child and that child was male, the results were an example of the rule of unintended consequences. Soon the females were in such short supply they became prized. That was not the original intention especially in some cultures. It was a curious even a hilarious outcome.

"But some men did not find it funny. There was only one woman to ten men, and so for a time more children could be allowed each woman. But the competition for women was so enormous, that women became greatly revered, put on a pedestal, and came to control the planet. The females came to rule and in some areas polyandry was introduced. The Matriarchy became the norm on Earth but that was a century ago."

"The matriarchy was unconcerned with the out migration to other planets. The excess men sometimes went alone, but this was a sterile migration. Sometimes the migrants were allowed to bring female egg cells to be grown for mating outside the womb on another world. But no one who left the solar system was allowed to return."

Andy continued, hoping he was not telling the Root too much about humans. "The matriarchy on Earth continued to produce both males and females, but always many more males, so as to further their original power and control. The need for women on Earth led to a cult and female domination."

"The opposite of the problem exists here on Eden," Andy went on, "for the men were the ones who ventured out into the wilds and were killed by the Chalda thorn. Yet I might have been able to beat the game back on Earth and Mars, find a mate, and have a regular family even in the matriarchal society that developed. I had my University education and family connections.

If the conspirators had not involved me in their hopeless cause and lied about me at the University on Mars, my life could have been different. The conspirator's lies caused the soldiers of the Empire to come after me and I fled."

"It takes a male and female to mate?" The words drifted to him slowly. The plant was in no hurry. "Please explain human the mating process."

Andy Mars felt no embarrassment with the question to the plant. He was coolly descriptive. Sex education for a plant! "The females had the eggs and should have been prized and sought after anyway," the Great Root declared. "It is strange. So the population on Earth should have declined with such rigid control."

"Yes. In theory. Actually there are so many different ways to cheat, even now, that the population has become largely static at fifty billion. This is really about an ultimate number for Earth. And the situation keeps changing. A hundred thousand people every year migrate to the outworlds. But that is not enough to reduce or change the population of Earth. A hundred space transports leave Earth every year, two each week, each with a thousand passengers, and it does not affect the population of Earth at all. Most people who want to leave can go, if they are able to pay the fare. The fares are very high. On Mars, since it is a major outbound base, it is even easier to leave."

"Is there enough food for so many humans on Earth?" "The Earth still supports its people. The farming is much different than it is here. There are giant machines. There has been climate control for centuries. The rainfall is modified by the winds to fall only in the middle of the night. The rainfall comes at night automatically here on Eden, because of the winds and the high central mountains. The whole of farming is computerized on Earth.

On this planet, Eden, the populations are still small, a few thousand in their separate villages. Our Eden village is called Plymouth, after an ancient Earth colony. There are a dozen other villages up and down this one roaring river, places that have all been given Biblical or ancient names: Lebanon, New Jerusalem, Jordan, Bethlehem, and others. Each village has plenty of land around for farming. And most of this planet is still pretty wild. So even with the little machinery we have and the primitive methods, there is still more food per person growing naturally than on Earth."

"So you were a spacer in what you call your second life. Tell me about that." The plant was curious. And knowledge is power. How much should he tell the plant? Yet he owed the Root his very existence. If there were hidden motives here, then so be it. He had promised to help the Root in some way. He was wondering what would be expected of him and did not ask, yet. The Root had helped save his life. Andy hoped the price would not be too high.

"Eventually I became a Captain of space freighters and also space passenger ships. I explored beyond the rim of the known planets whenever I could. There were many stories. There were tall tales of the wonder worlds, the youth planets, where time was extended or went backwards, where men lived forever, where the only danger was staying too long and becoming too young. These were absurd tales of infants crawling and seeking a womb and women fleeing. There was talk that those on such planets were keeping it a secret so as not to be overrun by immigrants, even complaining about the environment so as to frighten visitors and tourists away."

"These stories I heard and tried to check out as I navigated the trade routes. I was satisfied to see old people creeping about on all the planets I visited and wrote the whole idea off as myth. Perhaps I will try again someday."

"Humans live longer than their domesticated animals," the Great Root stated. "Is that a condition for domestication?"

"I don't know," Andy admitted. How had the Great Root discovered these things? Perhaps the sheep and chickens of the Pilgrims had been observed.

"We were talking of traveling to the stars," Andy continued. "What was not myth was what was termed 'jetlag,' on Earth in the long ago, and this problem was compounded when you visited many planets. Each world had its own cycle of days and years and the body took weeks to adjust."

It was why Andy enjoyed Eden, with its high oxygen content, its smaller size and lower gravity, even its five moons, small, but never out of sight. He looked up now, seeing three of the five moons, dimmed but visible even in the midday sun. The joke was that when people on Eden said "many moons" they were not talking of time, but rather a condition.

Andy paused, reflecting, remembering how going in and out of warp drive as a navigator became a strain on even a healthy young man. He had adapted better than most.

Then Andy Mars thought of his training at Sanctuary, the predictions there, and other things he would not tell the Root just yet. Perhaps that training had also helped save him from death by the Chalda Thorn. The Chalda was still a mystery, and he must ask the Root for information. He was now thinking of "the Great Root" as his friend and promised to return soon.

3

THE NAVIGATOR OF THE STARS

....

As he made his way back from conversing with the Great Root, Andy Mars reflected again on his adventures as a navigator of the stars. He had been first running away from the Empire and from the University on Mars. As a navigator Andy first pretended more than he knew and then knew more than he pretended. As a navigator he had treasured the star maps and all the information he could obtain as he became Captain of huge vessels.

"Tell me about your space travel?" came the telepathic words from the Root when Andy Mars returned the next day. Andy related some of what he knew. And some he did not tell. There had been a time in the early centuries when space travel was at ten per cent of the speed of light. The early spacers, the true explorers of those days gave their lives gladly. They went into 'static sleep' to make a journey of sixty or eighty or even two hundred years, in order to reach the very nearest stars, and some never awakened. There were long journeys and often those trips found nothing. Robot ships had gone first, but those explorations were not always accurate in what they reported back. Some who embarked on the longer trips awakened landed only to find an Earth colony already established by ships that possessed the light drive. It was quite a shock.

The light drive systems had come next and were still improving. These ships used a series of jumps once a ship was beyond a sun system, truly removed from the pressure of much visible matter. In the early light drive days the attraction of another star system often pulled the jumping ships right in to huge suns to their death. The star maps were so necessary and sometimes pilots falsified them with codes to send others to their doom. But men learned. Even now there was still much to be discovered about space navigation. Just as the most valuable tool to the first navigators of the Earth's oceans were maps and charts, so the star maps were the most important things in the work of the space navigators.

At one time men sat on the piers of Earth staring at the endless oceans and wondering at the fabled monsters that lay beyond. How could one ever cross such an expanse of water? Ferdinand Magellan's ships that first sailed around the world, took three years. Then the voyages became commonplace and finally were reduced to hours by planes and later to minutes by space ships.

Just as men sat on the piers staring at the wide oceans, they had stood on platform Earth and stared into their telescopes at the unreachable stars. But once out beyond the solar system, past the pull of gravity of their sun, the physics changed.

The Light Drive led to "The Grand Migration." The adventurous sought freedom of every kind; their own idea of utopia was to be discovered; their own version of civilizations on new planets was the goal. Now as the Empire expanded, the thousand freedoms, on as many planets, seemed to be in danger.

The Confederation of Planets gave way to the Empire, but there was always the infinite beyond. Men had explored only a bit of just their own galaxy, even now. The over one hundred million stars in this Milky Way galaxy alone seemed enough forever.

Only the Empire was spreading, seizing control, and establishing its dominance within this region. Of course the free worlds were not perfect either. They were unable to band together against the Empire, because they were so different, one from another and they insisted upon fighting each other.

And finally the force fields offered a way to protect the planets, so that people could live in peace on each world, if they could afford the enormous cost of a security force field. Earth had covered itself with such a shield, for protection against the Empire, but the Empire was interested in the outer worlds, not in Mother Earth. Long ago the major nations of Earth had installed national force fields around their borders to prevent attack. Even small breakaway cultural groups had established tiny countries, sometimes enclaves within another country and its force shield, and erected their own protection. The force screens do not allow objects the size of people or planes through, but the atmosphere can circulate.

Andy Mars, as a navigator and finally a Captain of the huge star ships, had avoided trips going to the Empire. His most interesting times were spent in the ports on the Free Planets, where he enjoyed the Cafes at the edge of the galaxy. Here the tall tales were told and the wild yarns. He had heard of the Holy Ones, the future-tellers, the sooth-sayers, the predictors, and the Mystics.

Once he had gone purposely and alone to the planet called "Sanctuary" in search of the fabled "Monastery of Peace" with its "Golden Pavilion." He had traveled out into the endless desert on that planet by skim car, with maps that were perhaps in error. It was part lark and part a need to know the mystery. The huge pillared golden castle was screened, but not force shielded. He buzzed in slowly through the wide-open metal gates and landed in the courtyard, surprised to be admitted so easily. Then Andy had a feeling his coming was expected and the leaders here had been anticipating his arrival.

The man who met him in the enormous courtyard had the "look": he was a person of bearing, a young man, assured, solemn, yet not pretentious. He was dressed simply in a white cloak and soft trousers. His face was that of a hawk, ready to strike. "We were awaiting you," he declared. It seemed like a good line, but it might be real.

"And I have come," Andy Mars replied giving nothing away.

"I am Kalin, the one who serves. Before you can meet the Master, the Mystic One, you must go through me."

"I will be glad to talk to you Kalin. Going through might be more difficult." Andy laughed easily.

"Yes, but it is just that. The training is needed and I can begin it."

"You were speaking exactly. I must go through you."

Andy smiled narrowly now.

"I will give you training."

"I am at your disposal."

"This is the art of combat for the living," Kalin declared. "Better than the dead," Andy replied. He was strong and fast, but wished now he had practiced more of the old martial arts still taught by some in the classes at the University on Mars. Still Andy was not without some skills. He had not only smashed the two armed Imperial Guards who came to arrest him so long ago on Mars, he had done the job quickly and easily.

"You have no weapon and I none either," Kalin observed. "Come at me; we will practice."

"I do not fear you, but do not hate you either," Andy confided. "I came merely seeking information."

"And you will receive knowledge of a sort in turn. Come, we will practice." Kalin smiled patiently. He seemed annoyingly certain of himself.

Andy rushed him, expecting the trap, counting on his agility and strength and yet he seemed to pass through, and fall down. The white gravel stones where he landed were hard. Kalin stood waiting.

Andy arose and smiled ruefully. "You are good," Andy admitted. "I can not even analyze how you did that."

"Try again, slowly. I have no secrets from you. You are one we can use or you can use us. The galaxy is before you."

Andy came in slowly, hands out but arms bent, looking for a contact. He would use strength and not speed this time. Again he seemed to pass through. This time he did not fall, but he felt clumsy. He half expected nothing to grasp; though it was difficult to accustom himself to the idea that he would feel nothing as he reached out and sought contact."

"Are you a holograph?" Andy inquired.

"No, I am here, even as you are."

"And again, even more slowly," Andy requested. His very speed had been used against him and his strength turned away with ease.

This time Andy moved as in a dream, in slow motion, seeking, and he found contact. Now he held Kalin, and then his adversary was no longer there. "It is in the mind," Kalin declared. "You are good. You touched me."

"I did more than touch; I gripped you. Yet you eluded me," Andy admitted ruefully. "You do have knowledge I could use."

"The first time you tried speed, and you are very fast. The second time you tried strength, of which you have more of than I. But the third time you used your mind and moved very well. You will learn quickly."

"This fighting is fine, until someone sees you from afar with a fragmentation finger pistol which you do not notice in time."

"The noticing is all important," Kalin retorted. "This is the art of escape. It is evasion, until you decide what to do with your opponent."

"It is no fast introduction," Andy Mars agreed. "Going through you will take time. I would like to learn more."

"We have a school. You are qualified to stay here and receive instruction. Soon you will move to higher levels."

And so Andy Mars was assigned a small hut. There were apparently no dues, no request for funds. The Master, or the Mystic One, was not in evidence. But Andy Mars enjoyed being in the fraternity of the Monastery of Peace. There were over a hundred others here, mostly young, nearly all men, and seekers. They were not so much outcasts as devout in their desire to learn. They wore white garb, soft trousers, shirts, and cloaks with a hood as Kalin did. Andy made friends, but he let it be known that he did not expect to stay long or join the priesthood.

He practiced with the other "chosen ones" who were seeking answers as he was, but perhaps not the same answers. Too soon one day he left the group standing in their rows waiting and walked up to Kalin, his hand outstretched. "Will you shake hands with me?" Andy asked. Kalin smiled. "Yes. We will be friends. The Mystic One says that you are one of the anointed and someday you will rise above us all."

Andy gripped Kalin's hand stoutly and he was held tightly in turn. Then he began to try to twist to little avail.

"You offered a hand in friendship, but now instead you test me," Kalin declared. Suddenly Kalin was not quite there. Andy was holding nothing. None of the acolytes behind him laughed.

"It is not a trick, but a state of mind," Kalin explained. "There is a removal of oneself from assault."

"I have much to learn," Andy confessed.

"I am a sensitive, but not on the order of the Mystic One."

"Tell me about the Mystic One, Kalin?"

"There are gifts. People first must have faith and believe. The Mystic One can see. How do you describe a new sense to one who does not have it? How do you explain seeing to one who is blind?"

"So I am yet blind. When will I see?"

And then in the castle behind them the wide golden doors opened for the first time that Andy had seen. A slender man of merely medium size, old, white of beard, wearing a blue cape stepped out on the stone entranceway: "We never learn it all, Andy Mars. But you need to become an adept. Yet know this, it is a real world. Not fantasy. You are destined to be a player in a great galactic game. It is not prescribed yet that you will win or lose, but Kalin may teach you enough to stay alive and enter the lists of the future. Kalin is beyond the adepts. He has been genetically altered."

Andy stood marveling at the words, understanding he was in the presence of the "Mystic One." Then the man was gone, not in a puff of smoke, but just no longer there. And Andy saw that Kalin and all the acolytes behind him were bowing very low.

There was indeed much to learn.

*   *   *

The practice was more than using the speed and strength of an opponent against him, though that was a beginning. Andy was so large and strong that this concept was difficult for him. He was a member of the second circle of adepts. Andy felt he could just smash them if necessary, so removing himself from combat seemed almost a waste and was hard to learn. The inner circle, the adepts, those who had been here studying for many months or years, this was quite another matter. They could not be reached; even coming up behind them quietly was impossible. These advanced students had learned.

The respect for the inner circle was easy to give willingly. This was not quite a military organization, but there was the camaraderie, a friendship, a bonding of fellowship. The relaxation techniques, the meditation, the mind leaving the body were all well known ancient ways, combined here in a mystical shadow dancing, "a dreaming streaming" some called it. What was the purpose? The lessons were worth learning. Andy stayed on, becoming especially friends with Brian Winthrop. Brian was a tall, lanky fellow, with a square face and almost yellow hair. His cheek and forehead had interesting scars he did not talk about.

Andy had left his own scar on his right cheek obtained when he fought the two Imperial Guards on Mars. But why had Brian not covered his much more obvious scars in an era when any skin or body graft was possible. Andy never asked.

Brian was of the inner circle. He had fled the Empire, studied in the Free Worlds, and when Andy inquired, Brian was forthright enough: "I am obviously looking for something." He laughed very heartily, enjoying a joke on himself. "It would be nice to know what I was looking for. But that is enough about me. As to where this school, this institution of the adepts is leading, I do not know. The Mystic One does somehow see beyond.

He knew you were coming. You are somehow important and fit into the scheme of things to come."

"And you?" Andy asked his new friend.

"I am more of a plodder. You have heard of the Guardians?"

"Yes. Not much," Andy replied suddenly understanding some things that were whispered about in the galaxy among the star navigators. "The Guardians have been used as teams to keep peace on the Free Planets," Andy spoke what he knew or had heard. "But they are a small group, hundreds. They can not match the Empire in any way."

"Nor will they," Brian replied. "Still this is not a new idea. There is a long tradition of peacekeepers, of Swiss Guards in the deep past on Earth, of those who try to save humanity from itself. You will have to ask Kalin for more or perhaps the Mystic One the next time he speaks." Brian laughed. The expectation was you did not inquire of the Mystic One.

Slowly the art of the impossible, removing oneself from the combat and allowing the opponent to simply grasp at nothing became second nature. There was also the awareness, the sensing of danger or problems, even those things that were about to happen. Andy learned so fast that he amazed all but Kalin who seemed to have expected it. After four months Andy joined the inner circle.

Recently a group of new recruits had come in and a platoon of the inner circle had moved out as Guardians to watch over a minor war between two of the Free Planets.

Then there was the day Andy once more tried his skills against Kalin. The two were alone in the great courtyard, maneuvering without touching for an hour. At last Andy's concentration broke and he found Kalin behind him, waiting. And Andy then asked Kalin: "The Mystic One says you were genetically altered. What was done?"

"I was chosen at birth. I have five small hearts down the center of my chest that beat in rotation. If one wears out, it can be replaced easily. There were other modifications."

Before Andy could inquire further the doors of the Golden Pavilion opened at that moment and the "Mystic One" appeared once more.

"You are in a hurry to move on, Andy Mars," the Mystic One declared. "While it is true you have now learned the basics, there is always more. There will be a time when you will call on us. The Empire is stretching its tentacles out everywhere and could even reach here eventually. And the Empire will come to the next place you call home, unless we find a way to prevent it. I feel you have decided to leave us soon. We are a small group, and alone can do little against the millions in the army of the Empire. But the galaxy is open to change."

And Andy brought himself to ask a question about the Guardians: "How do the Guardians fit into this future scheme?"

The Mystic One stood, almost an apparition, perhaps a projection, wavering on the steps of the Pavilion, his white cloak and scarf seeming to blow on the wind on this calm day. "Andy Mars know this. The myth is that wars have reasons, that men fight because they are attacked, that somehow by wishing peace or protesting, as they still do on the Free Planets, that all men can solve the problems that cause conflict. Men have always been aggressive."

The Mystic one continued: "Without that aggressive quality men would still be picking berries back on Earth. Men have moved from dominance of their own planet to the control of many. Even those who protest against wars are merely satisfying their own aggressive needs. Their protests satisfy their own war fever. They will not admit to their own aggression. We here on Sanctuary can only move with the winds to provide security. You go to do what you must. Call on us at the time that is coming."

Then the Mystic One was gone. The doors of the Pavilion closed again.

4

THE PILGRIMS

"What brought you here as a spacer?" the Great Root inquired when Andy Mars returned once more to the edge of the clearing the next day.

"I met my best wife, Myra, whose family had been persecuted by the Empire for little reason. At least this is the story, to hear her tell it. It is a common tale." And Andy privately thought: There is a secret here about Myra, a mystery she conceals about her early life she never talks of and somehow I must not ask.

Then Andy Mars thought of Myra in the house on the hill, not a kilometer from here. Myra was small as Andy was huge; narrow as he was wide; soft as he was hard; yet she too was a seeker looking for something. And small as she was, Myra was voluptuous. She kept her beautiful curves hidden under clothing, as required by the Pilgrims. This hiding her beauty did not seem to bother Myra.

He and Myra seemed to talk forever and it was good talk, but at times they seemed to talk around things and not into them. The space voyage to Eden had been a good place for endless talk. Andy taught her his biology and she learned more rapidly than he expected. She was bright and willing. He saw her as an equal and loved her mightily.

It was Myra who had told Andy of the Pilgrims and they had joined them. Andy felt he had enough of bring a space navigator for now; the long voyages between the stars had been too much. He hoped to farm. But he soon wished also to think and decide about these Pilgrims. The starship they came on was a freighter which the Pilgrims called "the Ark" though its real name was a prosaic "X-D77." The Pilgrims probably had the better name for the ship.

The Pilgrims were looking for God in Space, a seeking that was a hunger. Their theory, as set forth in their blessed book: "The Journey through Space and Time," was simple enough. If they could get out beyond the speed of light to that time when Christ had not yet been born on Earth, they could become original Christians again. Some few wanted to alter time, to prevent the Crucifixion itself, while others felt that to perform this "anti-miracle" mankind would not then be saved.

There was much more. The Pilgrim's Holy Book was convoluted; an enormous original set of theories. Andy reserved judgment on the whole matter. The Pilgrims had come as far as their money would take them. The Pilgrims were angry about many things. The change of universal dates bothered them. This year was counted as Earth standard year 547 ASA, After the Space Age. The change ignored the whole Christian calendar. The Pilgrims desired, as with the early American Pilgrims who went to Massachusetts in America, to light a beacon for mankind. So these Pilgrims had gone first to Mars and there attempted to use Time Travel to go back to the time of Christ.

The Time Travel Institute on Mars had ended that Pilgrim dream by refusing them. The Institute did not allow group travel. Time Travel was a curious study, anyway. Historians of the deep past were the most acceptable time travelers. But the leaders of the Institute had become fearful of the corruption of the timeline. The charge for using Time Travel was very expensive. Further, the Institute had demanded that people who wished to go back and visit a certain era learn the languages involved and make a study of the period.

At first the 'time tourists' had to wear a wrist band that indicated any corrupting influence they might be causing. As long as the wristband remained blue, the travelers had not changed the timeline. With the slightest color deviation, the travelers were to return at once.

Of course if they created an entirely new timeline they were beyond any return at all, then the travelers were in their own dimensional multiverse. The difficulty was, even with solitary historians, there were always those secretly dissatisfied with some segment of the past and wished to alter the timeline.

When some time tourists did not return at all, there was concern. So a completely foolproof method had been developed by the Institute. Time tourists had to return the day before they left, which proved the timeline had not been corrupted. If you did not return before you left, you would not be sent back. The conundrum joke, told by those who laughed at the Time Travel Institute, was that the process was like getting up before you went to bed to see if you slept.

Cosmologists, those scientists who studied the universe, questioned if time and space and even reality were real. They still debated endless theories, new and old, all without ultimate answers. Andy believed you had to accept this reality or you would bump into a door or run your starship into a sun. Anyway the Pilgrims had been refused and left Mars. Andy caught up with them at a later space jump point. Andy thought the Pilgrim time travel effort was ridiculous, but Eden sounded like an interesting planet to Myra and the Pilgrim ideas could be tolerated.

There were other people already on Eden when the Pilgrims arrived, a scattering of earlier settlers, people who had taken up residence on the other continents or on the other side of the high mountains. There was plenty of room for the Pilgrims on half a small continent.

Only life here on Eden was very different than the Pilgrims had imagined or their Holy Book suggested.

Eden had less than ten per cent of the land area of old Earth, yet all the oceans, lakes, and seas, were fresh water.

There were huge ten kilometer high mountains, a backbone for the continents. All of the continents were curved as scimitars, long and narrow. The rains fell in torrential sheets down the high mountains, turning into streams and smaller waterways that divided the land everywhere as the rivers ran into the oceans.

Andy Mars and his wife Myra had come with the Pilgrims. They turned their small savings into provisions for the house on the hill, four kilometers from the Pilgrim village but near other Pilgrim farms.

The house on the hill already had a history. It was a house of death, which some of the Pilgrims feared. It was built originally for one of the Pilgrim Prophets, a man who had argued with the Church hierarchy and gone to live apart from the village. This Prophet's plan had been to cause others to come to him, to build houses around him and create a new village. Religions were always splitting. Instead this Prophet was soon stung by the Chalda Thorn and died. The Pilgrims felt that God had spoken and he was a false prophet. The house was empty and the price to buy it reasonable.

This outland world named Eden seemed to Andy to offer a chance to settle down to real happiness. Closer to Earth the Empire was growing and controlling more worlds. The Emperor ignored the beehives of crowded Earth. He seized only the star systems that seemed most valuable in the outer regions. Here on Eden there was no admonition against childbirth. There was a balance between the sexes again on the planets away from Earth. Then the Chalda Thorn had presented very different problems.

The Root interrupted Andy's thoughts, asking another question: "When you arrived here, you a biologist, burned off the vegetation around your house with blasters. Why?"

"Yes, it was ugly thing I did," Andy admitted. Perhaps it was best to pacify the Root. Andy shrugged. "I turned everything brown for a thousand-meter circle around the house. I had been told of the Chalda Thorn. Many men have died of it here. Indeed the culture of this planet is the opposite of Earth. The holy book of the Pilgrims says men must work and women bear children. The religion of the Pilgrims says they must multiply and flourish, which is why they left Earth."

"The population control on Earth was distasteful to them," Andy continued. "Many people who left Earth made several space jumps. Those on new planets usually achieved a balance of the sexes in a generation. But the Pilgrims left with enough female converts. On their arrival on this planet, which they named Eden, the men largely became farmers. There are some craftsmen, who built the homes and furnishings. Carpentry was especially allowed and admired. But the farming here is still primitive by Earth's standards and keeps most men occupied."

"The Chalda Thorn has been killing the men while the surplus women are entered into plural marriage so that the word of God may be spread. The women are to reproduce, which requires husbands. To my Myra's annoyance, I have been forced to take on two other wives, Felicity and Happy. Although Myra has been strangely accepting. I have also been forced to pretend a conversion to the Pilgrim faith, for the sake of peace. Otherwise they would continue to come to preach at me to fulfill what they see as their duty to convert me."

"So you have lied to them and pretended a conversion you do not believe?"

It was hard to be honest about lying. "Yes. I wanted peace. I wanted to be left alone. It was not a right thing I did, but I did not have strong feelings on the matter. It may be the Pilgrims are right in their beliefs."

"Tell me about your farming? Why did you plant alien seeds?" Andy Mars felt he was being called into judgement by this Root. He related his efforts, explaining how he had examined the ground carefully and taken soil samples. In the valley below were berries, fruits, and nuts that could be eaten, according to the early settlers. He had planted seeds from Earth, but they had not grown well. He began gathering a harvest of native plants that would be sold to the spacecraft that came through once monthly. But there was little profit in this. Carefully he explored the jumbled jungle of plants outside the perimeter, until he could recognize easily the Chalda vines with their telltale three-cornered, triangle-shaped leaves and their deadly thorns.

It was interesting to think of this Eden in terms of the original Garden of Eden on Earth, for now he was helping the Pilgrims give names to the new plants. It was good to be first and give a name to new things as Adam had done. In places the vegetation was unbelievably thick. Andy dressed with heavy clothing and gloves even though the temperature was tropical, toward off a possible sting of the Chalda.

Andy Mars was worried about one thing. The Root had declared it wished him to help, and now that he had survived, he must deliver that help. He owed. What form would the request of the Great Root take? He was in the word of the Pilgrims, beholding to this plant. He did not know if he should remind the Root of this help to which he had agreed.

Instead he asked: "What shall I call you?"

"I see the word 'Root' in your mind, Andy Mars. It also means 'basic thing' in your language. 'Root' is fine. You can call me what you wish. The name will not change me, as it does with humans. I am more than my name."

Andy could stand it no longer. He needed to know what the Root wanted of him. What had he promised, when he believed he would die? He was standing, with his shirt off, his bare hairy chest against the mother Root, his elbows on its knar, his arms extended, talking aloud to a plant and no longer feeling foolish in doing so.

"What do you want of me? Do you want my help in destroying other competing plants?" He could get out his blaster and …

Suddenly he had the shakes again, for an instant, and while this was a passing response, it was almost as if the Great Root had laughed.

Then after a pause Andy felt the words from the Great Root again: "First, you must go to the Pilgrim Village and warn them. They have blasted one of my roots with their weapons and burned it away. Yet they use my roots to walk over, as a bridge to ford streams and rivers. It may be my root was in their way, but they can build steps over me and we can live in harmony. If it happens again, I shall take action against them." The open ended threat was the most severe, Andy decided. When you do not explain exactly what you may do, it seems much worse.

His task was easy enough, if the Pilgrims would listen. "And what else?" Andy inquired.

The Root did not always seem to speak directly, but wandered about. "Animals have the advantage of being more ambulatory, Andy Mars. They pick up and go. But plants to move and travel, even if more slowly. Their stems and branches move over the ground. The roots of plants move above ground or below. And now I will tell you an important secret Andy Mars: All of life desires to expand their kind."

Andy returned to his original theme. "Do you need some help against other plants somewhere on this planet?"

"No." The Root's laughter returned to shake him. "If I wished, there is no other plant on this planet I could not destroy by myself, though it would take time. I live in balance, in harmony, and while the other plants unconsciously fight each other, I allow them to exist. I repel rather than destroy when they attack me. My power here is absolute."

"How do the plants fight?" Andy inquired, knowing, yet wishing to hear what the Great Root might say. "In many ways. By shading each other with thick leaves and depriving another of sunlight. By actual struggle with roots grappling below ground. By drinking the water faster than a neighboring plant and gradually limiting the action of others around them. My favorite is to simply infiltrate and take over, boring into the roots of neighboring plants and subverting them. Soon I am them and they are a part of me."

A sudden thought occurred and Andy Mars spoke aloud:

"Are there many of your kind? I see your trees at the edge of the meadow grassland where I walked once on the far side of the village. I see them also along the ocean shore fifty kilometers from here." Could the Root want help with its own kind?

"They are me. I am one. Once there were many, but we joined and subsumed. We are a unity of oneness. We traverse the vast oceans, and are on all three of the continents: this one which you call the Big Continent, and the smaller ones which your people call the North Continent and the South Continent."

"Your roots run along under the ocean floor then?"

"Yes. I am one."

"Why do you not destroy the Chalda Thorn?"

"The Chalda does not bother me or most other plants. It has developed only in the last few thousand years. It has killed some of the birds, though they usually flutter only to the high tree branches. But the Chalda has killed all the in between animals except for the river lizards who do not venture beyond the stream banks out of choice."

The Great Root seemed to sense Andy Mar's consternation and paused. "No, I perceive your feeling. The death of all the animals seemed senseless to me, but I did not interfere. It was a natural order of things."

"There are quite of variety of bugs on Eden," Andy observed, "some insects almost ten centimeters long, but they did not evolve with humans and so they don't sting or bite us or go after our crops."

Evolution took differing paths on each planet, Andy decided. It depended on the atmosphere, gravity, water, and the life that appeared. Man had grown up on Earth and was molded by that planet.

Then he had another thought: "You seem to have become many plants, all attached to your roots."

The Great Root paused for a bit, and then continued. "I am many and one. I am trees and shrubs, vines and grasslands. I have experimented with biology myself. Since I am predominant, I grew into all kinds of plants. I ran root systems underground to form flowers and match all kinds of plants. Gradually we all became one. I can be any plant as long as it is connected to my roots."

Andy took a deep breath. "Tell me more about the river lizards," he asked.

"The river lizards enjoy the cool mud and are a satisfied species who believe in the simple life. Perhaps it is because they do not have your fingers to manipulate things. I have my vines, but have never felt the need for artifacts either. Yet the river lizards are as intelligent as men. They do not disclose themselves to men. They wish to be left alone, and men find them not good to eat. They have altered themselves so that will be the case."

The lizards as an intelligent species was a shocker. Andy decided he would have to investigate the river lizards later. For a moment he thrust this new information aside, because suddenly he saw an important truth. One of the major mysteries of the planet Eden fell into place. In the thousands of rivers were the long-bodied river lizards, larger than humans. Their skin, if it could be called that, was lumpy and green as an Earthly alligator. The lizards ate the abundant fish, and seemed to live happily along the riverbanks. The question some Pilgrims had asked was, why were there not more land animals, more in between species leading to these large lizards. But the Chalda Thorn had killed the other land animals and the in between species.

There was so much to think about here. "Tell me more of the river lizards," Andy requested.

"I have sharpened my sensations to the microscopic and the telescopic," the Great Root declared. "I have no eyes, but yet I see. I learned seeing by talking to the lizards and then being invited into their minds and using their eyes. They taught me much including how to eventually communicate with you. Finally it was the river lizards that told me of the constant influx from space of the spoors of microorganisms. They had discovered this without seeing it. The seeds of life drift down from space to all the planets, seeking habitable worlds and changing to meet conditions, if they survive at all. Life then is expansion, it is seeking, it is aggrandizing."

"There is then only life and non-life," Andy Mars ventured. "You do not ascribe intelligence to non-life, though I have seen people who trip and fall cry out "damn rock" which apparently relegates the rock to an inferior place in the afterlife. This is beyond my understanding. Life includes animals and vegetation. Why not intelligence to vegetation such as myself?"

Andy laughed: "Human prejudice."

But what had the Root said about manipulating things? He reflected. Was the Great Root telling the whole truth? Could a plant lie? A plant could probably not move fast enough to manipulate things except very slowly. A sudden amusing picture formed in Andy's mind, a picture of a plant in a pot with vines, sitting in the pilot seat of a starship, seatbelt attached, and flying off on an adventure. Andy Mars thrust the thought from his mind.

He had to know the rest: "Tell me, what is the main thing that you wish of me? How am I to pay my debt?"

"You have survived. You are healthier now than before your sting. Do you realize your sense of wellbeing is not because of communion with me, but from having partaken of the Chalda Thorn? I can sense the continuing Chalda presence in your body."

Information. Interesting. But not the answer to the question. Why did the Root not tell him directly what it wanted? Probably because it could not force him to do its bidding. "Tell me please," Andy Mars asked again.

"You will aid me in a number of ways." The Root made it sound certain. "It is symbiosis," the Root continued. "I wish to spread my seeds among the planets. You have access to space ships. You have a saying from back on Earth, one that I see in your mind, which is very illustrative: 'A chicken is just an egg's way of making another egg.'"

Andy chuckled. It was a joke. But more seriously, this plant, this root, wished to visit the planets of the stars! No, it was more than a visit. The Root wished to spread to other worlds. Would Andy be a traitor to all of mankind if he arranged such a thing? Yet he had promised. A thought came to Andy. "Have you tried before to spread beyond this planet?" he asked.

"Have you noticed, Andy Mars, the clouds of seeds that sweep the space station on the days the galactic star freighters are due in port?"

Yes he had noticed. "You were trying to spread your seeds to the stars."

"Yes. I am probably a relatively immortal creature on this planet. To not know if I am getting into any containers, attaching to any of the crew's clothing, this is somehow a thankless and sad venture. My seeds are scattered on the winds of chance."

"It is a lonely endeavor," Andy agreed. "You do not know what happens to your seeds. But why do you want to spread your progeny?" It was a silly question and Andy knew this even as he asked.

"Why does any animal, any plant, any life, want to expand?
It is the first element that distinguishes life from non-life."

"You are answering a question with a question?"

"Instinct. But to further this instinct in animals led to thought. I have sensors. All other plants spread out blindly. There would be no life, animal or vegetation, without the inbred need to spread out. Here is something I have wondered about, Andy. I have observed the river lizards and then the humans. The humans are very secretive about your sexual relations. I am unisexual. I feel no passion. I send out my seeds at the spaceport. I can change my genetic code for myself or for my seeds. But what conditions may my seeds find on other worlds? And then I thought, is that not the situation for humans as well? It is unacknowledged, perhaps, not thought through."

"What do you mean?" Andy inquired.

"Humans have children. Then they try to train them, to teach them, to impart knowledge. Finally they send them out in the world alone. And the worst thing is you do not know what conditions your children may find in the future."

"That is true."

"But another matter, one I hesitate to touch on."

It was Andy's turn to laugh. "Go ahead. Anything goes. We are friends."

"All right. It is this human passion, love, well I have a problem with it."

"There is love on many levels. Love for a home, a place, or a pleasing possession. If humans seem to be great collectors it is perhaps a struggle for permanence in a world that ends too soon for them. There is love for children, parents, spouses."

"All right. Is human sexual love, passion, any more than the covered over need to procreate?"

How to answer that? Andy shrugged. "You take away the glory, the romance, the high adventure. Most of our novels deal with love or war or both."

"You are all short term creatures, you humans," the Great Root declared sadly. "Only immortality for you would produce disastrous results. There would be overcrowding beyond your ability to curtail. But massive increases in your life span would have the same result. I could be a plant pharmacist with ease, creating, dispensing." The

Great Root paused. "We will speak of this more another time," the Root concluded.

They talked further and Andy Mars left with a feeling of empathy with this plant.

*   *   *

Another thought loomed in the mind of Andy Mars. He was feeling better, stronger, and more energetic than he remembered ever feeling before, now that he had recovered from the poison of the Chalda Thorn. He needed to analyze the Chalda poison. A whole arena of ideas opened to him. Andy did not yet see that he had grasped an idea that would change the very nature of his world.

Andy had several theories as to why he was alive, when everyone else who had been stung by the Chalda had died. First, he had not been fully injected by the Chalda Thorn, so the amount of poison he had received had been minimal while other men received a full sting. Second, he was stronger, larger in body than most men, and therefore more likely to survive. Third, the wisdom he had learned while a student at Sanctuary had aided him in trying to remove his body from poison. Finally the plant root had definitely greatly helped.

Which of these was primary? Did he really owe the Great Root anything? Yet he had promised and would keep his word.

No one had ever gotten a pincers and really plucked a Chalda Thorn to examine it. That was something he must do.

Another problem was how could he keep the first part of his bargain and prevent the Pilgrims from blasting the root that crossed their fields? Yes, they could build steps over the root, but that would be inconvenient. Yet the root helped the Pilgrims by acting as a natural bridge across streams and rivers. Symbiosis again. Man had always elevated himself, taking what he wanted from nature, not seeing what nature gave to him. If the Pilgrims thought something was against their religion, they would never accept it. He had to make this demand of the Great Root seem natural and within the concepts of the Pilgrim religion.

Andy inquired of the Root: "Will you communicate with other men, if I bring them here? It will help in convincing them."

"Perhaps, one or two people. I do not want large crowds." crowd was defined as more than two plus Andy! Amusing.

"This will all take time," Andy warned. "I have made a promise and I shall try to keep it."

"Time I have more of than you. The arrival of humans on this planet presents the greatest challenge I have ever had since my early days. You are an honest man, Andy Mars. I wondered when your people landed, what they would do about the Chalda. If they decided to devastate the whole planet to rid themselves of the thorn, then I would have had to deal with them."

How old was the Great Root? Was it appropriate to ask? He did so anyway. "How old are you?"

"I do not know. I was here ages before I was aware of time and further ages before I communicated with the river lizards and began to think of other matters." Andy decided that self-awareness was the beginning of thought and of being.

"I wish to experiment upon the Chalda Thorn," Andy declared. "Perhaps I can offer the Pilgrims something they can not resist. I will return to talk to you more."

5

THE CHALDA THORN ELIXER

Andy Mars returned to the house on the hill full of thought. He had told no one of his communication with the Great Root, certainly not the Pilgrims, not Felicity, who could be trusted with a secret, not Happy, who bubbled out all she knew, not even his best wife, Myra, with whom he shared his council on all other matters, Myra his greatest love.

There were seven rooms in the house on the hill, a kitchen, a meeting room, a communication room, and three bedrooms. There was one spare room, which was almost ominous, used for storage so far. His wives each had a bedroom, and as yet they had no children. The decision was his, he knew, for all of his wives were ready. But the Pilgrims had not complained as yet that he was not following the 'Word' to be fruitful.

That night he slept with Myra, his best wife, who had accepted this state of affairs, his multiple wives, but often talked of the two of them beginning their travels again and going to another planet. She talked that way only in the quiet of her own bedroom when they were alone.

Myra was such a tiny mite, and yet so bright. She had soaked in all the biology he could teach her and even wanted to know about the navigation of the starships. Now she told him quite simply: "The

Pilgrims regard you with awe. They feel you are blessed for having survived the Chalda sting, and this is an important sign. Up to this point the House on the Hill where we live was regarded as evil because of the false prophet who came here and died. But now you are regarded as having the potential to be a leader, a Prophet yourself." She had been visiting the village again.

"Because I survived the Chalda Thorn?"

"Yes. They had us all as widows already and were deciding whom we should marry next. This is the danger, if we stay on this cursed planet. I will be handed off to some fanatic I care nothing for. And I will have to flee. I want you to teach me more about star ship navigation. Why do the books on the subject have so many gaps?"

Andy laughed. "Because the navigators do not want too much competition. You would be regarded as too small, but there was a time in the early days when tiny was perfect."

"Why? Explain that?"

"The first ships that went beyond the solar system had weight limits. They especially wanted forty kilo women and sixty kilo men, tops."

The women with their delicate hands for fixing things were especially important, and Myra was a perfect forty, almost exactly forty kilos.

When he met Myra, she had money of her own, more credits saved than he, earned she said at jobs to seek out a new life. All their money had gone into the house and the farming equipment.

*   *   *

The day was half again as long on Eden as men were accustomed to on old Earth, but the hours had been altered to ninety minutes. There were no seasons, neither the equator nor the poles could be defined, and the days were universally warm and tropical throughout the year. Men took a long nap in the early afternoon, at the hottest time, and now with the end-day stretching endlessly before him,

Andy Mars set forth with a backpack of tools to obtain a sample of the Chalda Thorn. Already some really wild ideas were forming in his mind. He must see what was truly possible.

His wives had all bid him be careful, and he certainly intended to be cautious. For a bit he stood just outside the house, surveying the area of the hill he had blasted, the tarpaulin covered farm equipment, and sniffed the air for a possible end-day rain. It was humid, but the cumulus clouds seemed white and withdrawn above the looming mountains in the distance. It usually rained only at night. Someday he would explore those mountain peaks too.

Along the pathway he had planted some of the jungle flowers that blossomed in their odd colors, blacks, greens, and pale yellows. He followed the path down toward the jungle, examining as he went. Here he had blasted deeper, at a Chalda plant, and there was nothing left.

He moved in to the thick, high grass now, safe here where the Chalda never grew. The grasslands had squeezed everything out. The Great Root was correct, the plants warred too against each other, in a slow, silent battle, roots fighting underground, branches vying for sunlight, squeezing other plants out by shading them.

Now Andy Mars entered the thick wooded vine country, cutting his way through carefully with his blaster. It would sure not do to hit one of the Great Root's offshoots. There ahead, attached to a tall tree, winding about in profusion, were the green triangle leaves of the Chalda, thorns concealed behind the leaves, hanging down to sting anything in its path. Why was it so deadly and what was its secret?

He approached cautiously from the side. Overhead, stretching upward, other Chalda hung, draped between trees, hanging like ornamental decorations. The Pilgrims carried pictures of early Christmas trees on Earth, with hanging tinsel and ropes of silver and gold dangling from the branches. This view reminded him of those pictures.

Andy Mars looked about carefully. Gently he snipped the leaves away that almost hid a half-meter thorn he had selected. Soon the thorn stood out as sharply as a naked needle, pointed at him, waiting for its moment. Then he put on his metallic gloves and tried to cut the vine itself on both sides of this thorn. The vine was a three centimeter thick monster, and he squeezed hard on the pinchers. At last it snapped with a violent shudder that shook all the greenery.

He let go of the vine and jumped back as it fell clear, in an arc, almost as if it aimed at him. Bending over, Andy held the vine with the thorn and prepared to snip the other side. Again it required a lot of pressure. The snap created a new shudder and abruptly one of the upper vines fell upon him and a Chalda Thorn pierced his heavy shirt and stung him full on the back.

Andy fell flat at the blow. This was no scratch, but the full injection of the poison in back of his shoulder. He would have but seconds to live and there was no hope! His enormous strength, further communion with the Great Root, nothing could save him now!

* * *

So many thoughts, in delirium and death. An accident was what happened when you were not careful enough. How stupid to have this occur twice. He deserved to die. There were those Chalda vines suspended overhead, and it never occurred to him they might fall when he cut the vine below. Those who had died of the Chalda Thorn had not come back to tell why they had been stung, what stupid mistakes they had made. They never explained the errors that led to their death.

The vine had not really fallen, but been set to spring at him. Yet he had noted this spring action before and still was led into the trap. The Pilgrims would see it as a judgement.

The vine was motivated by some homing instinct that sent it down to kill when the plant was disturbed.

Andy reached back and the Chalda Thorn, which was so tough to cut had actually pulled loose and was lodged deeply in his back. He tried weakly to pull the thorn from his shoulder, but it felt slippery and was fully imbedded. The thorn was like a dagger thrust into his flesh.

He tried to think. There was always something to do, even when you have but moments to live. He was still alive, so he should pick up the other thorn he had cut, wrap it in his bag and return to the house to die. A second time! How stupid he was. Most men finished their dying the first time.

But perhaps ... And then the saving thought came. Yes, that was it. With the full dose of poison injected this time, he should have been dead in seconds. Perhaps the first scratch by the Chalda and his recovery had made him partially immune. With the full injection, he actually did not feel as stricken as the first time.

He could return to the Great Root for help. No. He would not confess his stupidity at being stung a second time to the Great Root. Live or die this time, he would battle it out himself alone.

For a long time Andy Mars lay where he had fallen. He felt the fever come and the sweat. Yet he was not dead. It had to be that he had adapted due to his first scratch by the Chalda Thorn. After a bit he arose, picked up the thorn on the ground he had snipped from the lower vine, and walked back slowly to the House on the Hill.

His wives saw him coming up the path. Again they ran out to help him, Felicity and Happy standing back when they saw the Thorn. He was a man who could return with the Chalda Thorn stuck right in his shoulder. He was a man of miracles. He was a Saint, blessed. They fell on their knees on each side of him and began praying.

Myra shrieked when she saw the thorn, and then became angry, demanding that Felicity and Happy help. Yet neither would touch Andy, but followed the two back to the house their heads bowed. It was Myra who took off the backpack, carefully around the thorn. It was Myra who found a pliers and pulled the thorn from his back to lay it upon the table.

The three then helped him to bed again.

*   *   *

This time Andy's fever was not as high or his time in bed as long. When the word spread as to his encounter with the Chalda, the

Pilgrims from the village came out and walked around the house on the hill, praying quietly, as they circled, all twelve hundred of them, women carrying babies, men with their heads bowed. Andy Mars was a living miracle.

Happy added to the effect by taking the long thorn, which she had personally seen imbedded in Andy's back, and placing it carefully with a pliers on a pillow. She carried the thorn out for all to view with awe as they passed in their praying circle. Happy told what she had seen, a man returning with the Chalda Thorn plunged deep into his back, repeating the story again and again for all that would listen.

On the third day Andy Mars was up. On the fourth day he was ready to experiment on the Chalda Thorn he had snipped from the vine. First he walked to the village and purchased a young sheep, which was grazing in the enclosed meadow.

When Andy Mars cut into the Chalda Thorn, he found it contained almost two cups of black poison. The experiment was simple. He took an eyedropper and removed only two drops of the poison. These two drops he placed in a full liter of water and shook well. Then he took a spoonful of this water and fed the sheep. Even with only a spoonful, the sheep became quite ill. For three days Andy was afraid he had killed the sheep. Then the fever broke.

After seven days he fed the sheep two spoonfuls of the elixir. The sheep did not get sick this time. It too was immune. At the end of a week he tried a full drop of the poison on the animal. The sheep survived this too showing no ill effect at all.

Now Andy made the first capsules of the Chalda Elixir. He began with a liter of water and just two drops of the Chalda poison. Shake well. Then he made capsules. He asked for a volunteer. His three wives were fearful, but all volunteered. He selected Happy and trustingly she took the capsule.

Even with such a small dose, he had almost gone too far. Happy became ill for the customary three days. She too would be immune to the Chalda. He increased the dosage and she did not become ill again. He would have to begin with still smaller doses and then continue with larger amounts.

Andy made up capsules and carried them to the village. It was Bishop Jacob Swife, a sturdy leader of the Pilgrim hierarchy that he went to see. The Bishop had a large house and five wives. He did no farming and scarcely left the village, so he was in no danger from the Chalda Thorn. The Bishop was an elderly rotund man, sparse of hair and large of nose. It seemed to Andy that the Bishop partook a bit too much of the holy wine. But that was not Andy's business.

The Bishop was glad to be called upon by the famous Andy Mars who had survived the Chalda Thorn twice. But what Andy was about to tell him was even more startling. There was a way to prevent the frequent deaths by the Chalda Thorn which had killed so many of the men. The people of the village should take the capsules he had prepared.

The Bishop suggested Andy present the matter to the congregation at the evening assembly the next day. A high-steepled church, which would be fitting for the Pilgrims, was being built in the village. But temporarily the townspeople gathered in the central square of the village and the leaders of the church ascended a platform where they stood or sat upon some wooden chairs. Since it was warm in their tropical Eden, they only had to schedule their meetings in the early evening time before the nightly rain.

The townspeople gathered, a study in brown garb, as they sat on the grassy meadow of the village square. It was interesting to Andy that throughout human civilization there had been designated costumes. The Pilgrims all wore a plain brown to show they were not sinfully showing off finery. Still this lack of costuming was in itself a costume. After the formal prayers, Andy was introduced.

Andy Mars spoke from the heart: "You all know that I was twice stung by the Chalda Thorn. The first time I almost died, but was spared." Andy paused. It would not hurt to make his survival a little bit of a miracle yet. He had a selling job to do and wanted no problems.

"The second time the thorn was imbedded in my back. Yet I survived. This time my survival was partly because I had become immune to the poison. I have prepared some capsules, which I would like some volunteers to take. They have a very tiny dose of the Chalda. If you become slightly ill, you must rest. In a week, you take two capsules and then in another week three. My belief is that you will develop immunity to the Chalda Thorn so that if you are stung, you will survive. Even the women should eventually take the capsules, for Chastity Hagan was stung by the Chalda just two days ago as she walked the path from her farm to the village."

There was a buzz of conversation. Prudence Conrad stood up to declare: "Chastity wandered from the true path to the village. The fault was her own. Chastity was misnamed and we all know why she was struck down."

"None of us should judge, else we be judged," Bishop Swife declared silenced Prudence. "All of us are capable of error." There was a rumor in the village that Chastity was not being exactly chaste when she left the village on the day she died. But she had died.

There was not only fear, but some other questions. "How much do the capsules cost?" one large fellow, Simon Semple, asked.

"They are free. I have made these for the people of this village because I wish to help." The questioning about costs ceased. Then Matt Davis stood to protest. "This is Eden and you wish to make it perfect. But the Chalda Thorn was put here to test us and weed out the impure. I have farmed further into the jungle than any, with caution it is true, but without ill effect. We must not interfere with the tests of God." Matt Davis was a large man with a powerful voice.

It abruptly occurred to Andy that one could not fathom human behavior. "Some men might desire the gambling roulette of the Chalda Thorn so they can obtain additional wives when the unwary or unlucky are killed," Andy Mars suggested.

Matt Davis was holding his spade as if it were a symbol of his devotion to the soil. He flushed now at these words and rushed at Andy, the spade held on high. For the first time on Eden Andy used the techniques he had learned on Sanctuary from the Guardians. Matt found himself lying on the grass on the other side of Andy. He had apparently run right through him. There was a murmur of a miracle among the group.

"Miracle nothing," Matt Davis growled, rising to swing the spade. Again he missed and fell, even though to the beholders it seemed he had passed right through Andy Mars. "Those who wish to volunteer can try," Andy declared, turning his back on the man on the ground. "I want only ten men who have courage and will promise to follow directions."

Now Simon Semple stood again, his muscular arms folded on his wide chest. "I believe in you, Andy Mars. I shall volunteer."

Others followed. Andy had his ten volunteers. For three weeks he stayed all day in the village, watching those who had volunteered. The dose was so small now, that no one developed a fever. The second week there was no effect from two capsules, and none from the three capsules on the third week.

Then the fourth week, Simon Semple was out farming and was struck badly by a Chalda Thorn. He was sick for a day, but recovered quickly. Everyone wanted the capsules of Andy Mars now. Even Matt Davis asked to be included. The women too sought the capsules.

There were a number of other questions Andy had. Would the immunity to the Chalda fade? The best answer was to take one capsule a week forever. Soon an unexpected fringe benefit became apparent in taking the Chalda Elixir. Andy Mars and all the people who began taking the elixir felt better. They did not suffer as much from the tropical diseases of the planet. The very buzzing insects left them alone. There was a change in the blood chemistry. Andy described his own feelings in naturalistic terms: It was like warm sunlight and gentle rain. Suddenly Andy Mars saw his discovery as one that transcended the danger of the Chalda Thorns and might be valuable off the planet.

6

THE PLANT GOD

Andy Mars continued to have long talks with the Great Root. Finally he decided upon a fresh course of action. Andy primed the Root as to what to say, and brought to the forest glade two of the major Pilgrim Elders: the Prophet Howard Wenzel and Bishop Jacob Swife. They were fearful of the Chalda Thorn, but Andy assured them that they would not enter the jungle at all, merely view the Great Root from a safe region.

The Elders agreed reluctantly and at last they arrived.

"This is a sacred place," Andy declared. He waved his arm to encompass all: the wide open grassland behind them they had walked across, the hundred meter high trees to the right and left, the wild untamed jungle ahead, and the Great Root stretching out far over the hills on each side.

The two church leaders looked at each other. They would have considered such remarks blasphemy, if they had come from anyone else than the famous Andy Mars who had survived the Chalda Thorn. "Stand just here and pray," Andy suggested. Prophet Howard was one who prayed loudly, perhaps so all would know how holy he was. He was taller than the Bishop, but thin and gray. The Prophet possessed a long white beard, a bit scrawny, hair that blew in the wind just now. His beard never hung quite straight down but always shifted from one side to the other as if it were alive. He was often argumentative and his favorite phrase seemed to be: "Let me tell you why you are wrong." The Bishop, though older, seemed with his ruddy cheeks and sleekly rotund body to be fuller of life than Prophet Howard.

Abruptly as they stood there the words entered the minds of Andy and the other two men. "You are welcome here to this holy place." Bishop Swife stood with his mouth open and Prophet Howard for once was speechless.

"You have heard?" Andy inquired.

"This is my servant, Andy Mars, whom I consider blessed." came the voice inside their heads.

Andy bowed in humility, though he had asked the Great Root to say just this. Prophet Howard moved the tall grasses in front of him aside carefully and studied the area. "I hear a voice," he admitted in confusion. "It is inside my head.

This is not a public address system or microphones. I have put my hands over my ears and yet I heard."

Oh, if you could only pray that way, Andy thought.

"I too felt the words," indicated the Bishop. "Who are you that speaks to us?" the Bishop asked. "Is this communication coming from the big vine here? Are we being addressed by a plant?"

"I am the one you have sought in traveling to this planet," came the words. "I have communicated often with Andy Mars. My desire is that now since you have won against the Chalda Thorn that you come to live in peace with all animals and plants on this world. There are plenty of grasslands to be cleared for farming and grazing your flocks. You must not blast the Great Roots such as you see before you now. This must not happen any longer. In some regions you Pilgrims already use these roots for bridges across streams and rivers. What helps you must not be injured. You must live in harmony with nature."

Andy was concerned that the Bishop and Prophet would back so far away from the Root in fright that they would be out of range. They kept retreating.

"Stay where you are. Do not move further back from this sacred communication," Andy requested.

"The Great Roots on this planet are holy and not to be blasted," the words inside the three human's heads continued. "This must be communicated to all men, or men may not be allowed to remain on this planet."

"How does this conversation happen?" the Prophet asked aloud. "The vine is awake and aware. It is a miracle." Abruptly, as if each decided simultaneously, the Bishop and Prophet fell on their knees. "It is a sign, a manifestation. This is the Plant God," declared the Prophet.

After a bit more discussion the Bishop and Prophet readily agreed to the Root's request. "May we bring the congregation back to this sacred place to hear the word?" the Bishop inquired. "This is curious. It is as if there were something holy here, but it is a plant."

"No," Andy Mars advised. "This is only for the elders of our church, you who are most holy." This caused the Bishop to smile and the Prophet had a twinkle in his eye. The statement was easy for them to believe and well received.

"We did not exactly come to this planet to find this root ..." the Bishop began, his voice trailing off.

"But we knew there was a reason we came here," the Prophet declared. "Somehow this planet was ordained. Moses saw God in a burning bush. This is a Plant God!"

"You must spread this message to the rest of the congregation," the Great Root concluded.

And Andy Mars felt that he had at least completed part of his promise to the Root.

* * *

In the next weeks the Pilgrim leaders designed Andy Mars as a Prophet. If that was necessary to move forward, he accepted the title. He felt no glory in the name. The Pilgrims had their ways. At least the blasting of the Great Roots became off limits. So far so good.

But Andy Mars moved into danger when he traveled to Dethilm, the capital of the Empire. When the Empire retaliated, all was lost. But that was yet to come.

* * *

In the meantime the communication with the Great Root began to result in increasingly happy changes. Standing in the forest primeval, next to the open cleared meadow, Andy talked long to the Great Root. The Root inquired about man's needs. "Now that I have reached a unitary feeling for people, I can adjust the plants and flower colors to please your eyes and nose as on Earth." The Great Root paused, and then returned to that subject.

"One curiosity, Andy Mars. I have listened to people talking as they crossed my root bridge that goes over the river near the capital at Lorraine. I find an odd human problem. You lose things. I suppose this is a problem with using things as humans do, instead of using extensions of myself as I do. You live in a world of things, clothes, games, ornamentation, toys, books, furniture, weapons, tools, paper lists and I am sure much more. You have collections I am not sure you need."

The Great Root stopped as if waiting for Andy to catch up. Then the Root continued: "Many times I have observed humans who were speaking of looking for things they misplaced. I need only soil, sun, and rain. Just as with the river lizards, I am content with life as it is. But you humans have brought new ideas to me, Andy Mars. I am enjoying the game we are playing right now."

Andy Mars merely laughed. "I am sure you find us strange."

The Great Root continued: "Humans cover themselves so only their head and hands show. But I have head woman talk on the bridge of the city of Lorraine of making up their face and people talk of facing the facts, putting a good face on things, and even of losing face. Some of this I don't understand yet. There are many puzzles."

There was a pause as Andy sought out a reply and then the Root inquired only more: "What is beauty, Andy Mars? I have asked you this before." It was a question right out of the books of the ancient philosophers, so easy to ask, so impossible to fully answer.

"Where did such a question even come from?" Andy replied in turn.

"Curiously enough it is a matter debated by the river lizards," the Great Root responded. "They have been my eyes in some ways. They have been my eyes and ears in some ways. For millenniums I lived in darkness, knowing only feeling, motion, the heat of the sun, the wind."

"And the river lizards are an intelligent species," Andy remembered. "I shall seek them out someday. But men have various concepts of beauty. Some say it is in the mind or eye of the beholder." Andy felt his answer too prosaic, too ordinary, not thought through. But he had not considered this idea of beauty much. So what is beauty to a blind man or to a plant he wondered?

"The fact is you humans have certain visual and auditory ranges,' the Great Root continued. "Is beauty therefore personal, but also species selected? Is there a universal beauty? You do not appreciate the ultra-violet beauty, for instance, because you cannot see it. But the river lizards can see this."

"Yes, there are beautiful sights, sounds, even smells," Andy agreed. "And these matters may vary with individual men. Few would argue with the beauty of a sunset, for instance," Andy proposed.

"So how can all men be pleased?"

"They can not. But there are agreements within certain limits. When I was on Earth I traveled to see types of agricultural stations but also I was interested in visiting some of the most famous art museums. There are pictures and genre of art I enjoy and appreciate more than others. A friend of mine declared once that you could tell the important paintings from the mediocre by where they were hung in the gallery. The famous picture had a room of its own with lights and space. The ordinary pictures were placed with others and grouped together. My friend was joking. But once decisions have been made that certain art is beautiful, the idea lingers for centuries. Few dare question these ideas of the so-called experts for fear of being called philistines." Andy thought about what he had just said. "Why do you ask?" he inquired.

"I want to know. I am asking people to leave my roots alone. My roots are not particularly beautiful. But I can cause vegetables and flowers to grow around them. I can simulate and produce. We can live in harmony."

"It sounds indeed like Eden," Andy Mars observed. And then he explained the human concept of paradise to the Root.

The Great Root followed through. Soon a profusion of flowers and green plants began to grow in cascades of ornamentation, each producing a perfume that filled the air with scents beyond belief. The plants the Pilgrims grew for food developed to an optimum height for harvesting and became more productive.

More and more the Pilgrims began to speak with reverence of the Plant God.

*   *   *

There were so many next steps, all of which could go wrong, that Andy Mars felt almost overwhelmed. His first life was a student on Mars; his second a navigator of the stars, culminating with his discovery of Sanctuary and learning under the Mystic One. He had viewed his third life as that of a humble farmer on Eden, practicing his biology, learning about the strange new plants on this virgin planet, and living with Myra, his great love.

Now, abruptly the human galaxy beyond Eden opened before him. There were opportunities and also enormous dangers. Here was obviously a chance for a fourth life, that of Merchant Prince. But he must be cautious and try to win one battle at a time. He was trying to take the long view. Andy felt he was being driven by forces beyond him into an inevitable battle with the Empire which he could only lose. Were events really predestined, beyond any efforts that men could actually exert, as the Pilgrims believed?

In the village Simon Semple had taken to following him around, trying to find things to do to help Andy Mars. One day Andy talked to Simon directly while they both stood on the village dock at the riverfront. Here the raftsmen came downstream with their cargo, bound for what passed as the capital city of this planet, the town of Lorraine, located on the oceanfront.

"There are many books for leaders, Andy Mars," Simon suggested respectfully, "but no books for followers. You will need followers and must tell me what to do. You have what is called charisma and can make men wish to follow."

Simon was almost as tall as Andy and certainly as wide in the chest as Andy himself. But he seemed to shrink down before Andy, as if trying for subservience. Yet Simon possessed a prognathous jaw with a forward thrust that conveyed personality.

"Andy," Simon Semple declared, "my parents thought with our family last name that it was funny to give me a name that reminded many of a nursery rhythm that was old a thousand years ago. I guess it was funny when I was an infant and very young. But my name made a blight of my childhood, until I was too big for most men to quarrel with. But the name is right. I am a simple man. Still I see work to be done here and a place for me to help."

Andy smiled, his slow smile, which came on until it took over his whole face till he was almost radiant. When he was opposed, it seemed easy to try to persuade or to strike back. But Andy had difficulty with those in the village who wished to kneel down before him, to pray to him as a living Saint. Such humility upset him.

"Tell me why you say these things, Simon?" Andy asked.

"I can tell a leader, and I can see a man with a mission."

Andy looked Simon over. He was a plain man, his face rough, and he was dressed in the brown Pilgrim town garb. He wore the small tasseled cap that would have been pointed if it did not fall over and the brown thin short sleeved shirt. Yet his body seemed to bulge with strength under these quiet clothes. Now that the danger from the Chalda Thorn was over, the Pilgrims had begun to discard forever their heavy clothing worn while farming. The village brown was becoming the only clothing. Simon looked as if he would speak further and Andy Mars urged him: "Go on, Simon."

73

"I will tell you the truth Andy, and you can accept or reject me as you see fit," Simon replied after reflection. "I was a soldier in the army of the Emperor Alexius V. I know weapons. The first truth is that many good men I have laid to final rest. And I know not why. I fought not for a cause, but for a love of fighting. The Emperor had conquered the planet Glotan in the Sierra System. There was a need for a border outpost there to hold the planet between starship arrivals.

These Pilgrims here came in to Glotan and stayed for a time between spaceflights. They preached of Eden, which they regarded as paradise, and at the time they were trying to find this miracle home."

Simon paused and then went on: "I had my place, as a second in command, an officer of the Imperial Guards. Yet I deserted my post and left with the Pilgrims, on what they called their Ark, bound for Eden. The second truth is that I was never really converted by the Pilgrims, but rather I was looking for something I could believe in, some cause for my life. The soldiers of the Emperor are paid well. But that was not enough." Simon paused, reflecting. "I think this is a problem for many men in many ages. It is even a reason men join armies."

"You are trying to find yourself," Andy suggested.

"First you have to admit you are lost," Simon declared without emotion.

"I am standing on this dock, Simon, because I am going down river to the capital city of Lorraine, to the only spaceport on this planet. I want to sell my Chalda Thorn capsules in Lorraine and give some for trade to the spacemen. What I am doing is relegated to this planet."

"For now."

"For now," Andy agreed. Was Simon so Semple, as his name implied. He had been one of the Emperor's soldiers. Reputedly the Emperor Alexius V had spies on all the planets, to report on activities. The story of Andy Mars would be an open book in any case, if he followed the course he now considered. All would eventually know and see the situation developing. It was like a great galactic game of chess, and he could see only so many moves ahead.

The plan was simplicity itself: to sell the Chalda Elixir galaxy-wide and make so much money he could fence off this planet with force screens. Eventually that would mean competition with the Empire itself.

As if to mirror Andy's own thoughts, Simon asked: "I can see a vision in your eyes. May I come along on the river journey?"

"Yes, you may come. And yes, a vision is forming within my mind."

"The Empire is not all bad, Andy Mars," Simon ventured.

"You see much Simon. Good and Evil are not absolutes and often fool us."

7

THE RIVER RATS

Andy Mars and Simon Semple took a raft downriver to the port of Lorraine. For Andy it was a part of exploring the planet, understanding what Eden really was. When he had first arrived on this Plant Planet he and Myra had taken the motorized version of this trip, upriver, against the current, to the remote village where the Pilgrims had come to live. The rivers ran everywhere on Eden, and men made use of them. When he first arrived on the spacecraft, the Ark, with the Pilgrims, Andy had decided to join them, to move into a small village and try farming. Now the whole of this globe opened before him and the galaxy beyond.

Andy Mars and Simon Semple were on an open cargo and passenger raft crowded with people and goods all going to the Spaceport capital of Lorraine. The river was tricky, with many tributaries, as it coursed toward the ocean. Some of these rafts men had been here plying these rivers for many years before the Pilgrims came. The oarsmen thought of the Pilgrims as interlopers, even though the Pilgrims now outnumbered the original rough settlers of farm and town.

The passengers, mostly Pilgrims in their brown clothing, sat on the bolted down benches, watching, even clutching their belongings. The raft held about fifty people. As the vessel continued downstream, pushed along by a fast current, kept from the banks by three oarsmen with stout poles, Andy Mars became upset at the rear oarsmen's words. "Sit tight now, farmers, for this is the wild river. So hold on. You aren't sheering a sheep now, or planting a field."

The river ride was fast and the rapids splashed them, though sometimes the oarsmen seemed bent on making sure the passengers and cargo got a little wet. The Pilgrims sat huddled on the benches, crying out a bit when the spray struck them, but they appeared determined to put up with the antics of the oarsmen.

Finally Andy arose, grabbing a rope that was hanging down the center of the raft between two upright boards and he made his way to the back of the flat craft. He looked a moment at the lanky oarsman with his brown bony features and then Andy tried a little diplomacy: "Captain, it is beneath you to splash these people unnecessarily."

"Wrong, Pilgrim, on two counts," the rough young man replied. "I'm not a captain or even a mate on this raft, but just plain Skip Boyton, an oarsman. And nothing is beneath me. Besides, it's the river that is splashing these passengers."

"You want me to duck him, Andy?" The words came from Simon Semple who had followed Andy over to the back of the long raft. Andy had not been aware that Simon also had arisen.

The oarsman laughed. "And then who would steer this river cargo to Lorraine? Maybe, citizen, you would like to joust with oars in fair Lorraine this evening?"

"I'll joust with you, all right," Simon declared. "Just learn to steer this raft."

"It is settled," Skip Boyton concluded. "If you have the courage to help provide an evening's entertainment you be on the dock at seven this evening."

"My name is Simon. And I will be there."

To Andy it seemed that Simon wanted to prove himself or perhaps even more curious, to safeguard his leader, Andy Mars, from an adventure that was not fitting.

The river ride did seem to improve after this and there was less splashing of passengers. As they entered the dock area at the port of

Lorraine, Skip Boyton called out: "This evening at seven there will be a grand entertainment at the waterfront. The River Rats will put on a show, and one of your passengers, Simon, has volunteered to be given a bath by me."

"The river is cleaner than the oarsman," Simon called back. "It will be a shame to pollute it."

* * *

Eden was a rural planet, an agrarian sphere, a land of Pilgrims and planters. Even its villages and capital here at Lorraine were regions of one story homes, with the highest building in the outlying villages the churches. Here was a quiet world of unhurried people, hardworking, and zealous, independent humans, developing their way of existing.

Andy and Simon checked in at "The Lorraine," a new hotel, but still a rustic wooden hostelry built in the frontier style right at the waterfront. All the houses of Lorraine were of boards, cut from the trees of the planet, for imported materials brought in by starship were expensive. Andy hoped the wood was not from trees of the Great Root.

When Andy and Simon inquired of the innkeeper, a bald man standing behind his long counter, he got an earful as to the River Rats. "The oarsmen have their own company, Pilgrim. They put on a show at the riverfront docks several times a week and pass the hat among the viewers for compensation. But it is largely a show for their own entertainment. The River Rats are coarse, but necessary. For years they have jousted with their long poles. They enjoy baiting townsmen to participate, so they can duck them."

"So they are well practiced in the use of their poles?"

"Yes. There is a show this very evening."

"I will be part of their entertainment this evening," Simon spoke up. "I accepted a challenge."

The innkeeper looked sharply at the size of Simon. "You are strong enough, but it is the practice with the pole you do not have.

Two things, to give you a small chance, Pilgrim. First, the River Rats will never tell you, but if you notice, they all wear a leather brace over their left arm, with a leather cup attached. The end of the oar can fit into this cup and steady the blow, or else you will lose the pole first thing and then go flying into the river. Also make sure they pad the oar ends, as they do in their own practices with each other, or you can be badly injured. My own suspicion is that at the time of the joust, as they call it, the River Rats wear a shield of leather around their chest under their clothing, to carry the blow if they lose the joust."

"What is the nature of the contest?" It was the first time Simon seemed to realize what he had volunteered for.

"There is a saying on Eden that only a fool plays another man's game."

"All right, you have called me a fool," Simon growled. "Now tell me about the game."

"Small motorized rafts are used, of the kind that cross the river at Lorraine to the other side. They don't use the large rafts with passenger benches that go upriver. The small rafts go past each other at moderate speed, guided by one of the oarsmen. The other oarsman stands upright on the raft and jousts with his oar pole. The loser is dunked. There is a supply store right down the street for purchasing the leather arm brace and a cup to hold the pole that I recommended."

Andy and Simon checked into their hotel room and then visited the supply store, a nautical place, full of hanging nets for catching fish, poles for guiding rafts, fuel tanks, and yes, leather arm braces.

"You did this to protect me, Simon, but I do not think you need to go through with the combat," Andy advised.

"I gave my word," the former soldier responded stolidly.

"Words thrown out to a fool," Andy suggested.

"I was as much a fool as he," Simon returned.

Both Andy and Simon were dressed in the brown Pilgrim attire, and the rotund storekeeper was not helpful. He sold to the oarsmen and fishermen of the town, while Andy and Simon were merely one time customers, whom he cared little for. Andy asked: "You carry a leather vest to be worn in the jousting contests beneath your shirt?"

The storekeeper frowned. "Yes. How do you know about such matters?"

"Enough. We told you this man was going to enter the lists today. You should have told us more." They bought the vest for Simon too.

"We've spent too much of our little hard currency on this silly one time contest," Simon grumbled.

"There is only an hour before the event," Andy commented. "We will skip dinner and rent a raft to practice."

They found a little old man on the river front who rented rafts and offered to drive them about on the river. "You were bamboozled into accepting a challenge by one of the River Rats?" asked the old man.

"Yes," Simon admitted dubiously. Now this had become a contest not of strength, of which Simon had plenty, but of skill and practice in holding a long pole in the bobbing water of the river.

"Yes, I will be part of the evening's entertainment," Simon laughed. He turned to Andy. "When I trained for the Emperor's army, I did some high jumping, also pole vaulting with lighter poles than this, but poles, nevertheless," Simon reported. "I was too heavy, for the best pole vaulters are tall but light. I have never jousted, but I like the feel of poles. Still, I have never fought with these poles. We engaged in some of the archaic sword fighting in the guards, but that is not the same."

They practiced gripping the poles, Simon holding the end in the cup of the leather arm brace.

The docks of the riverfront harbor were becoming crowded with townspeople and visitors as the time for the contest approached. This was the only show in town. Andy and Simon watched the early contests, as the raftsmen drifted past each other, prodding with their poles, until one splashed into the drink. Then Skip Boyton came by to inquire: "Ready?" He had a pair of poles. "Yes," Simon agreed. "But all the other poles used by the oarsmen were padded till now. Those you offer me end in a spike."

"Ah, I thought you were a man of action." Skip laughed.

"You will joust with the same equipment the other River Rats employed," Andy demanded for Simon. "Or are you calling all the previous oarsmen cowards?"

"No," Skip backed down at this. "We will select padded poles, and you can choose which I shall use on your carcass."

They left the dock, Andy driving the small rented raft while Simon took his stance with the pole in the center. The two men talked as the craft moved out into the river. "We are going up river, and therefore will be slower than Skip Boyton's raft," Andy suggested. "Skip knows this. He has what is called home court advantage in sports. It is like playing a game of air skiing when the wind is against you. I must say this is one of the few individual contests still open to people."

"You're right," Simon agreed. "Space battles with star cruisers are over in seconds, sometimes before the enemy fleet is aware. There is often no individual valor there. Though I have observed some ways to even up such contests."

Andy considered this. There was more to Simon Semple than met the eye perhaps. Or maybe Andy was just too suspicious of everyone. Still, as the old saying had it, just because you are paranoid does not mean they are not out to get you.

Andy looked down river. Skip Boyton took the five-meter wooden pole and used it as a baton, clutching it in the center and twirling it about as he advanced down the waterway. He was demonstrating his virtuosity.

In Andy's judgment, Simon did not stand a chance. But the villager stood resolute, his pole out, waiting, knowing. "Sometimes, Andy, the battle is hopeless, and yet you play out the game."

Andy watched, guiding the raft, which was the easy part.

As the two rafts closed in, Skip swung his lance all about, to distract Simon, who remained fixed as a statue, waiting. Now they closed, and Skip's pole came down and across with a sudden smack at the end of Simon's pole, and the big man holding so tight to his paddle, lost his footing in the choppy water and went down on the raft surface. Still Simon clutched his oar.

"Arise, sir river knight," called Skip. "You have not had your proper dunking. Let us make another pass at it."

Simon picked himself up; moving his arms and legs to see if he were injured. "All right. One more time for your entertainment," he agreed.

Andy swung the craft about, as did Skip Boyton's driver. Simon was bending down at his feet, and as Andy watched, he saw that the big man was tying his feet to the log planking on the raft surface with rope. "If he hits you solidly, you will break both of your legs," Andy warned.

"Someone will," Simon growled savagely.

Skip had been waiting and now the two rafts moved toward each other. "We are going down river now," Andy declared. "The advantage is ours."

"It is only a slight advantage," Simon indicated. "Andy, as we close, give it full power, whatever that may be," Simon requested.

"All right." Andy was dubious and it showed in his voice.

The ships closed again. Andy gave the raft full power and headed right at the other craft. He would give the opposition something to think about. Would he pull away in time just to skirt pass or would they ram each other.

Simon stood resolute, but when Skip swung his pole, he hit Simon's pole and caught it directly. Simon's pole went flying and Simon stood apparently surprised without a weapon though still standing on the deck. Skip Boyton's pole came down hard aiming for Simon's midsection. Simon grabbed the end of Skip's pole, and quickly guided it to the side of his leather vest, till it caught in the cup on his arm, and holding tightly with both hands, pulled. Simon's feet tied to the logs held.

To Skip's surprise, the oarsman found himself borne off his feet, the pole still cupped to his arm. As the rafts collided the shock sent Skip right into the river, while Simon held his adversary's pole, swinging it aloft in triumph.

And Andy could not help noticing on the dock the other River Rats, laughing at Skip Boyton's discomfort.

*   *   *

Later that night, while Andy was binding Simon's bruised side in the hotel room, there was a knock on the door. It was Skip Boyton. The River Rat stood in the doorway, smiling. "I congratulate you. You won fair, though not quite square. You ought not to be able to cheat a man in the coin of his own country. But you managed well. You are no ordinary Pilgrims. I understand even that you are the famous Andy Mars who is about to save the planet from the Chalda Thorn. And you are Simon the Simple who cleaned up a bar in Lorraine on the way to becoming a Pilgrim in the backcountry. I have checked on you both, even though it is a little too late. Come down to our tavern and have a drink with all of us River Rats. The drinks will be on us."

And they did. Andy filed away this further interesting information on Simon. What was he really? The bar they went to was on the waterfront, built in an imagined old style of frontier bistros. The River Rats were a noisy bunch, drinking much and singing songs of the lore of the river. They had a cult of their own, which was not quite a religion as with the Pilgrims. The cult was expressed in a tale which began with the words: "First there was the river ..."

Amid many toasts Skip Boyton declared honestly: "If you ever need our help, Andy Mars, the River Rats will be there."

Simon was walking gingerly in the morning, his ankle aching, his side cut. "It was worth it," the former soldier told Andy. "So much fun I have not had for a long time."

8

THE MERCHANT OF THE STARS

....

When the next monthly star freighter arrived at the Spaceport of Lorraine the following day, Andy Mars gave a few of the Chalda pills to his friends among the navigation crew, enough to last the thirty days before their next return. He talked to Captain Harley James, a tough nut of a man, short, broad, with the shaven head of the spaceman. Only the small star attachment to his blue uniform indicated he was a captain. They met at the little restaurant, with all the windows looking out, in what passed for a space terminal here on Eden. The cargo was being unloaded and loaded by shuttle, since there was no force tube on this frontier planet.

"What manner of gift are these pills, Andy Mars?" Captain James demanded.

Andy would have to win over the captain or he could not make the next moves in this game at all. "They are an extract from the Chalda plant, a native concoction. They induce a sense of well being, without producing any intoxicating effect. There is no loss of motor skills. You simply take one a week. I am seriously thinking of marketing the product."

"Trading? Using my ship?"

"Exactly. The pills are small. You could haul millions without much of a problem." "And are they addictive? Do you have to have your fix? Once you take one, are you hooked with withdrawal symptoms if you don't do it every week? If my crew and I are guinea pigs for your experiment, will we be back next month desperate for more?"

Andy Mars frowned. He had been taking one a week for several weeks. What was addiction? He did not feel a need. There was no desire on his part to increase the dosage. Not yet. And he felt good. He said just that to the Captain.

"You know, Andy, one of the things we have had preached to us is the historical record. The Mesopotamians invented wine maybe six thousand B.S.A. The Egyptians invented beer maybe about the same time. The Europeans invented the retort and so distilled drinks maybe about one thousand B.S.A. Now in the hundreds of years since, we have had a good chance to find out what alcoholic drinks do to people and decide how much we want. They are knowns. Likewise with opium and some of the other drugs in recent centuries. But today we don't know what some of the strange drugs from new planets may do.

They are all illegal and people involved have had the Empire's wrath directed against them and ..." he left the sentence dangling, which was his trick. You never quite knew if the captain was finished speaking.

"Yes," Andy replied, "that's the one good thing about the Empire. It is the enforcement body in the outer worlds. The Earth lets its people go off to the stars in all directions if they can afford the ticket, and there are no questions asked."

Captain James looked about. "Don't speak against the Empire, Andy. You can get in the habit of doing this and make one slip which is overheard by the wrong people and ..." He made a sign of a finger across his throat. Then he added: "I trust you Andy Mars. You are all straight edges." It was one of the new phrases.

"The rule of one man and his court can produce instant decisions, is what I'm saying," Andy continued. "Some of the enforcements are good. The other planets often are debating societies, sometimes unable to agree on anything. It is the old argument between freedom and authority. Order, control, fast action lie on one side, while independence, liberty, the constant voting are on the other side. Democracy, the autocrats say, is just a choice between two bad men. As to this drug, I have been taking it for weeks and feel no dependence or need to increase the dosage. I don't believe I am addicted. Try four of these, one each week, before you return again and then give me your answer."

"And what will they wholesale for, when we need more?"

"One credit each. No more. And to your crew: Free, forever."

"My ship is the only one that stops at Eden. Remember that, Andy Mars. If things go wrong for my crew ..." Again the sentence and threat were unfinished.

* * *

The crew tried the pills, one each seven days as instructed. They were not warding off a possible encounter with Chalda Thorns in space, but they did feel better than they ever had without any loss of ability to perform their tasks. Curiously, along with a feeling of well being, certain varieties of space sickness seemed to be alleviated. When the star freighter returned in thirty days the crew wanted more and Captain James was willing to try to market some of the Chalda. Andy expected as much and had prepared ten thousand pills, bottled and for sale.

The word spread through the planets. Andy Mars was in business. The pills came in bottles of five, ten, and fifty.

The price was clearly marked on each bottle, one credit per pill. They could be marked up as a merchant might desire, but the original price was obvious. There was also the usual warning on the bottle: "This is sold as a health food only, not medication. Take one capsule a week. Do not exceed the recommended dose." The problem was, if people got to feeling good, then if one was pill was right, two might be better, and so on. Andy believed that five in a week at the start might produce illness and fever. It was the usual problem when dealing with the public. Some people were crazy. They might take

86

the whole bottle the first day and then complain or die. Aristotle's ancient dictum seemed apropos: "Moderation in everything," the ancient Greek had prescribed.

Andy had made himself and his wives the guinea pigs. He took the questions Captain Harley James had raised seriously, and stopped taking the Chalda pills for four weeks. He did not feel as well, the glow was gone, but he had no trouble quitting. There was no withdrawal, no adverse symptoms, and no problems. The test was a success. The Chalda pills were not addictive, at least for him. One trouble might be that people were different.

The next month on his following trip Captain James took one hundred thousand bottled Chalda Pills to market, and then the product took off. The Starships were the universal traders in the galaxy, bringing the produce of distant planets to market. Only Captain James greeting to Andy was disconcerting: "O.K. medicine man, you're going to be a winner," he had said. This greeting alluded to the old medicine men that went about the planets, selling dubious goods and leaving just before the law closed in. Andy Mars did not like the designation.

But soon Andy was selling to the star systems by the millions. At last the news reached Earth, a greater market by far than all the new star colonies combined. The order came in for ten million pills, then one hundred million, and within an Eden year, half the population of the little planet Eden was engaged in the drug trade, that is making Chalda capsules, and working for Andy Mars. Earth alone was importing ten billion Chalda pills a week.

*   *   *

Eden was a planet that revolved only slowly around its axis to form a long day and took 1122 of those days to complete a year. The Pilgrims kept their own week, for purposes of worship. The week was always a man created unit of time, artificial, unlike the day or the year. Of course the Pilgrims believed the week was divinely ordained. The

Pilgrims thought it was very significant that the doses of Chalda pill were to be taken once a week.

The production of the Chalda pill was broken down into its parts. At first the Chalda Thorns were merely gathered. Later the Chalda was planted in wide fields, with vines growing over poles or wires, much as grapes were cultivated. The thorns were snipped at the top to retain the fluid, and the poison emptied into containers. The mixture of the elixir was done at one main plant under careful laboratory conditions. The capsules, bottles, labels, and boxes were all made right on Eden.

Chemists on other planets tried to analyze the pill's contents to duplicate the Chalda Effect artificially so they might cut into the market. The chemists managed to come close at synthesis, but only at a far greater cost. The natural product was much cheaper so it was hard to compete with the Chalda Elixir from Eden.

The profits were astronomical for Andy Mars, the new Merchant Prince of Eden, but from the first he had realized that if he were successful he would be on a collision course with the powers of this galaxy. The Empire wanted control of every valuable venture.

Andy Mars was especially surprised at how, without any advertising except word of mouth, on a buying saturated planet such as Earth, the Chalda pills had still caught on. On Earth the advertising was so intense that people actually bought a necklace of "avoid waves" to ward off the advertising messages beamed at those out strolling on the ramps.

As business picked up Andy Mars entered what he now called the fourth stage of his life, that of Merchant Prince. The Pilgrims were not averse to becoming wealthy, and Andy shared his good fortune with the populace. The Pilgrims regarded their sudden success as God's will, as proof that they were right in their ways. How deeply Eden was in trouble was not fully apparent for a while.

The profits were rolling in, millions of universal credits, then billions, then trillions. Now Andy used the major banks of the Free Planets to conceal some of his wealth. The Chalda Elixir was sold cheaply, yet it was almost pure profit.

Ten billion people a week paying one credit for the Chalda ran the profits right off the scale. And the demand was increasing exponentially.

Intermediary traders, without repercussions so far, were selling the Chalda in the Empire as well.

* * *

There were so many things that happened simultaneously in the extended time that it took to build the Chalda business. Andy Mars oversaw the Chalda production, talked to the Great Root, explored the planet Eden, drank on occasion with the River Rats, and moved his family from the house on the hill in the country, to larger quarters in the planet capital, Lorraine.

His wives accepted the move, and Myra took charge of the main Chalda production plant. When they moved to the capital, Lorraine, still a little city, Myra said she would miss the local gossip of the small village of Plymouth. For instance, the big news on Andy's return from Lorraine had been that Prudence Higgins, one of the women of Plymouth, had been caught in adultery with another Pilgrim. Names indeed did not always follow true.

Myra did well managing the Chalda production; she knew more of chemistry than Andy had realized. It was good to have someone he could trust there, but Myra seemed at once to be glad to run such an industry and also wished to keep out of sight as much as possible in Lorraine. She remained a mystery.

As the Chalda business expanded, Andy received a visit from John Kent, the planetary governor. Kent suggested he wished to retire and Andy should take the job. John Kent had become an institution as governor of Eden, white-haired, and handsome, even in his old age. He was educated, cultured, one of the first on the planet in the early days, and then a convert to the Pilgrim cause. Some said he had converted too easily.

Andy Mars and John Kent met on the veranda of the Governor's House in Lorraine, and had lunch served on this terrace. "I am honored," Andy Mars declared, "but I really do not want your job."

"You are the man for the task," Governor John Kent declared. "You know there is not a lot of power here. The Pilgrims believe in the theocracy, the church run government. The government is to take care of crime and order. We have little crime and a lot of confusion which we call order." Kent smiled. "The Chalda has been a tremendous boon. Will the product continue to sell?"

"I hope so. I agree with you, this is a small planet. And I certainly believe in the less government the better."

"My own feeling exactly." said John Kent, who was so well known as to be called John of Lorraine on this planet. "I have always felt that Earth has too many laws. I have made a study of Earth as so many of us who were born off planet have. On Earth there are the world laws, the national laws, the provincial or state laws, the city ordinances, and no one but the legislative computers knows all the laws. The lawyers profit from excess laws, but not the people. I have joined the Pilgrims largely because I too believe in the simple life. I have always followed the dictum that a good law was one that got rid of two present laws."

"The bureaucracy of the Empire is growing to match the bureaucracy on Earth," Andy observed.

"Long ago it was proven that bureaucracies grow until they destroy. Where there is free food the vultures will gather. Bureaucracies add little to government with their endless statistics and studies. I am one of the few in government who has voluntarily cut his staff and salary. I feel you will be a good governor, Andy, because with the export of the Chalda you have enriched the planet, and you have enriched yourself. You do not need to dine at the public table. I have long been looking for a successor. We live further into old age these days, but our physical powers eventually fail."

Andy accepted being Governor of Eden, and bought a house next to the governor's mansion, insisting that John Kent of Lorraine live out his days in the government mansion itself.

9

THE RIVER LIZARDS

Andy Mars explored the planet Eden now by climbing some of the mountains, sailing the rivers in his own boat, and he even began trying to talk to the river lizard creatures. Many of the river lizards lay along the stream banks some distance from the town of Lorraine. The Root said they were an intelligent species. They swarm, lay about the riverbanks sometimes in groups and sometimes singly. Andy sat for some hours, the only human, talking aloud to the lizards, but no words of communication entered his head. The lizards did not seem to utter a sound or respond in any way. They were content to sit around him quietly.

Finally Andy returned to the Great Root for help with this puzzle of communication. "You wish to converse with the river lizards?" the Root asked. "Why?"

"Because they are there, I suppose. You said they are intelligent."

"It is the curiosity of humans that has caused them to be such a success. The lizards converse with antenna movements.

This creates a high tone you may not hear. Have you seen the four antennas that move above their heads? The lizards are similarly unaware of your vocal sounds as communication. Other large sea creatures in the oceans of Eden converse with eye movements and even tail flips in the sea. My under the ocean roots have noted these creatures, but while there is a great deal of communication, how could you ever reach them?"

"Are these fish intelligent, who communicate by the means you describe?" Andy asked.

"No. The river lizards are unique. They have thought deeply on life and especially this planet. I have learned much in conversing with them. You have moved to Lorraine, the capital, Andy Mars? It is perhaps inconvenient for you to return here?"

"I have bought my own boat, largely to return to the House on the Hill and go upriver in a few hours. I want to keep in contact with you, mainly."

"Do you see the area of my root you are standing before? Visualize it. Try to see a difference."

Andy examined it closely. The brown knarred root stood in front of him, as it emerged from the jungle clearing and then curving to return again to the jungle. It stood glistening in the sunlight. At first Andy saw nothing. Brown was brown. The Root was the Root. There were different whirls in the bark, but nothing significant. Then he noticed a slightly reddish cast to the Root coloring in the area where he now stood.

He was still puzzling over this when the Root spoke into his mind again: "Do you see any difference? Your primary sense is sight, followed closely by hearing. Mine is feeling and chemical, water, sun, soil. Communication between us is not easy."

"Perhaps the color. There is a reddish-brown glow."

"I can feel colors," related the Root. "I can feel and reproduce light wavelengths. Think hard on this color."

Andy concentrated.

"Now, can you find such a place as this elsewhere, near Lorraine, where I have proved useful in placing many roots across the river and formed low bridges that barges can slide under."

"Yes. Foot bridges. There has been talk of flattening the root tops and running vehicles. I have pressed for force craft, which will hover above the planet, rather than the expense of building roads. The hovercrafts are more costly but the road building is not cheap either."

"Look for what you call a reddish cast to my root near Lorraine. My sensors are there also. Indeed they are everywhere along my root, several every kilometer."

*　　*　　*

Back in the town of Lorraine, Andy Mars found the root bridges, high, curved upward in the center even, and the townspeople had worn down the top with their walking, although even the capital was not heavily populated on this frontier planet. On most other planets, Lorraine would have been considered a small city indeed.

For a time Andy studied the root, looking, and it all seemed the same. Then he noticed a reddish cast to the very bridge. This area was too well traveled to suit him. Next, following the root along, Andy found the same slight color variation a thousand meters down a branch root right at the Riverbank. Here the green river lizards also abounded, apparently resting, sitting atop the Great Root itself, their long tails curved at times or just stretching out.

Andy stood at this place and talked. There was no response. Nothing. He advanced on the Root and stood before it, only centimeters away. "Hello," he called.

"You are here. The lizards bid you welcome too."

Was the intelligence of the lizards real? Andy felt he was taking a lot on faith. Did the Great Root play jokes? Andy remembered a time when he was a small boy and his grandfather had claimed he could see through walls. His grandfather had proven his powers by describing the furniture in the next room, which of course his grandfather well knew in advance. It was a supposed joke upon a small boy, but it did not fool the small boy even at the time. The lizards did move their antenna. Was it really communication or was the Great Root having him on?

The Great Root had nerve centers or whatever was their equivalent, about every thousand meters. It could be listening to the talk of all the people who crossed its bridge. Was that in itself a threat to humans? How much could the Great Root learn by listening to people passing? Andy had expressed an interest in conversing with the lizards. Now what to say? How could he know if the conversation was real with the Root as intermediary? "Tell me about your species," Andy requested of the Root and through the Root to the lizards.

The words entered his mind and they were supposedly from the thoughts of the river lizards passed on by the Great Root. He would just have to take the Root's word for it. "We are quiet creatures. The river is good. The sun is good. The winds blow pleasantly. The soft mud is cool. The fish taste good. Conversation is good. Ideas are good. Teaching our young is good. Procreation is a necessity. We are satisfied." The Great Root elaborated on its own. Apparently the river lizards had all they wanted, a plentiful variety of fish to eat, fresh river water to drink and swim in, cool mud for a hot day, warm grasslands at the riverbanks, the sun.

"You have no contests, no games?"

"The young chase each other. They believe that is good. They seize a piece of wood and pull on it against each other. They try to swim fast. Some young ones slide over the waterfalls for good sport. We are interested in your species, Andy. Are your people all one as the Root, or are there individual differences as among our species? People run about with feverish activity and seemingly without purpose. Yet you build structures. You chose this planet to live upon. Is the temperature good and the climate pleasant here? It is warm. Why do you humans cover your bodies with clothes? What temperature do you desire?"

Here was enough to reply to for a while. Andy had a sudden picture in his mind of humans as seen by river lizards, a picture similar to Earth Ants, running in all directions without purpose or reason. At least that was the view of humans presented by this river lizard. Apparently. But did the ant on Earth really know what it was about in its running? Ants were so small people took little notice of them and people were so big the ants could not grasp them. Could the ants communicate with each other with their antenna as the river lizards? Andy wondered if he was talking to one river lizard or to many?

"Yes," Andy replied. He explained that Eden was a comfortable planet, and the temperature very pleasant. It was warm and the climate was constant with small variations during the day and night. Men wore clothes out of habit. On their home planet the climate varied. Originally men must have come from a warm, humid area of their planet Earth or a warm time period, else they would not have survived when they shed their fur. Then when the climate changed men wore animal skins. Now they wore clothes. Clothes often stood between man and man in understanding.

And Andy thought also, to himself that clothes were so many things. Symbolic. Shelter. Men hid behind them. They were a mask for the body. Were men afraid to discard their clothing on this perfect planet? Why did some humans consider their own kind who wore few clothes or no clothes to be savages?

In the original Eden, that the Pilgrims believed in so fervently, men and women had been naked and happy.

"Men do not live long and they do not seem to know contentment. Do they seek the good?" came the words from the Great Root, apparently relayed from the river lizards.

"How long do the river lizards live?" Andy asked.

"A thousand Eden years. Perhaps because we take it easy, basking in the sun, and we are contented in the good, friendly mud. Our lifestyle reduces our rate of metabolism. Of course the Great Root has lived longer than any of us. It takes things still easier." The Root seemed to laugh at this.

"I am a conduit now," the Root declared, "but I must pass on the words exactly or you will not trust me."

"All right. Enough," Andy declared. "The river lizards communicate by antenna vibration which they can all see. But you, Great Root, do not see them. How do you understand their communication?"

"Andy, the lizards feel the antenna vibrations as well as see them. People are in too much of a hurry. People rush by them and if by chance someone approaches with harmful intentions the lizards slide into the river. There are emanations they produce. I can teach you. But you must first open your mind to them."

"Open my mind? How do I do that?" Andy asked. He felt as if he were back on Sanctuary being instructed by the disciples of the Mystic One.

"I can feel their thoughts, Andy, and now that I have practiced I can sense your thoughts even over a distance. I did not want to say this to you before. But there are thoughts all about you. The Pilgrims brought their house pets, cats and dogs with them to Eden."

"No, the Pilgrims brought embryos of sheep, cows, cats, and dogs. Once they had decided Eden was going to be the planet where they would live, they began raising animals. The transport of animals was too costly. But there also were a limited number of embryos of each animal. In a way starting the raising of animals has pushed the Pilgrims into staying here. Of course they could start over with embryos, but that would be difficult."

"These pets think on a very low level," the Great Root interrupted. "Usually their thoughts deal with contentment and food. Often the pets think of smells as their primary sense."

"That is because their noses are often so close to the ground. Humans walking upright use their eyes and ears most. So you feel thoughts even among our domesticated animals?"

"The dogs seem to love some humans and the cats to love the place they are in. But the thoughts are there. I feel these thoughts when the dog pets are walked across my bridge logs. You are changing the subject, Andy. Now, open your mind, think. Above all wait. Close your eyes to restrict other outside perceptions."

Andy tried. Nothing seemed to happen. He could feel the wind blowing which was distracting. "I want to communicate with you river lizards directly," Andy spoke aloud. How could he tell if ideas that came to his mind were the Root or the lizards? Almost he laughed. Then he focused.

He felt first just inner peace, perhaps imagined. In the self and beyond the self. No, the Inner peace was real. He had never felt such contentment before. Andy tried to define it. That effort failed. Finally he tried to define the feelings he was receiving by exclusions. It was not the overwhelming glee of a fun party, not the chemical merriment of drinks with friends, just being at one with a multitude. The thoughts overlapped. They were confused at first and then easy to pick out. In an hour he was adept. He felt he was actually communicating with the river lizards.

But now Andy wondered what to say? Tell me about your philosophy, he could ask? The Great Root had said they were philosophical. That seemed an idle question. "Tell me more about your life?" Andy settled upon that mode of inquiry instead.

"We enjoy contemplating the good, the eternal and essential mysteries of the universe. We have not solved the riddles, but the Great Root says that humans have traveled much in the galaxy and you do not yet have complete answers either. There are those among us who believe an important leader is to come to us."

How many humans believed that for millenniums, Andy wondered? The Pilgrims would be interested in this communication, yet he better not pass this on. The Plant God, as they called the Great Root, was enough of a puzzle. To hear the Great Root translate from the river lizards or to receive thoughts from them was a bit too much.

"I am sorry that in the early days some of our people killed yours in an effort to obtain food," Andy offered. He had thought about ways of saying this, and decided he might as well just come out with it.

It was almost as if the lizard he was nearest to on the riverbank shrugged. Could he be beginning to understand them? "Your people did not know," came the reply. "Through an effort we made ourselves taste bad, and it has not happened again."

"Then you are masters of your own physiology?" Andy asked.

"Only to a certain extent." Andy wondered to what extent.

And then the one large river lizard he seemed to be talking to added: "The Root, as you call it, says humans have very short lives. They grow old quickly."

"Yes, compared to you lizards and the Great Root," Andy agreed.

Now Andy shrugged. There was nothing to do about it. The study of genetics had doubled the human life span in the last few centuries, and the Chalda Elixir might well extend existence even a bit further. Also the quality of old age had improved with new wonder drugs. But the time was never enough. "The individual dies, but the human race goes on," Andy offered.

"Yes, but is that enough for the individual? The Great Root tells us he has witnessed many human funerals. It is a ceremony, perhaps."

Many had died due to the Chalda Thorn, Andy reflected. But how did the Great Root know all this? "Yes, we have a ceremony at death," Andy replied. "And you?"

"When it is our time, we know. We say goodbye, and swim out into the ocean." And then the lizards changed the subject:

"What is time?" the lizard inquired. "Oh, I understand days, passages of sunlight and then the moon's bright light.

I understand the planet rotating around the sun, which you call a year. These events occur. But aside from that, what is time?"

Andy did not do well in his reply. Was the river lizard testing his intelligence? The lizard seemed to give up on this effort and changed the subject: "Tell us about other planets. Tell us of your space trips."

And Andy entered into what he hoped was a real conversation. He gladly talked about the stars and some of his trips.

The largest river lizard lying nearby on the mud bank asked: "Would you ever consider taking one of us along on a space ship to view the sights and report back to our People? We might even be able to suggest some things."

Andy had an image that was scarcely stranger than his previous view of a plant with its vines out, trying to fly a star ship. Here he saw in his mind the picture of a large river lizard in a tub with some fish as food, sitting before a viewing window. Andy decided it would not be a venture most ship captains would allow. But all life seeks expansion. Intelligent life tries to find means for doing so. The lizards lacked man's opposable thumb and fingers. They had long claws, but could not manipulate things.

"I do not possess a space craft of my own at the moment," Andy answered. "Maybe someday." Then he asked about the leadership of the lizards.

This seemed to be almost a foreign concept. "There are the young and the old," seemed to be about the best they could do.

"The young need instruction and there is much to learn if they wish to do so. Our species has a variety of types, just as you humans do."

Then the topic shifted to Andy's ideas on philosophy, cosmology, and the nature of the universe. Here was apparently a subject the river lizards often discussed among themselves and were much interested in.

Andy Mars told them many things he had learned in classes and then asked questions in turn.

While he did not even mention that subject, Andy wondered about thinking creatures and how many there might be that humans never discovered. Some intelligent life had been found on other planets, but no humanoids had been discovered. Humanoids were special. People grew up and were shaped by planet Earth. People were unique.

And none of the intelligent life on the other planets even approached what humans called civilization. But were the river lizards civilized? If the Great Root reported correctly, they certainly were. Did civilization consist of cities? There was a rule among humans not to settle on planets with thinking creatures, however primitive they might be, so as not to contaminate their culture. Now humans had inadvertently come to Eden without knowing there were intelligent species here. The humans would not leave. It was done.

Rene Descartes, the 17th century French philosopher, had declared: "I think; therefore I am." To Andy this always had meant that Descartes felt he had proven his self, reality, and existence by thought. It was akin to the other philosophic conundrum: "If there is no man in a forest, a falling tree will make no sound." That meant again that men were the measure of all things. Men were the center of the universe to judge all, if that idea was followed. But a falling tree produced vibrations, even if no human was there to call it a noise or a sound. Could thinking lizards prove their existence the same way? Was the Great Root there because it thought? Did that mean a radish, an unthinking vegetable, was not there?

After a while the Great Root cut in and made it clear it was speaking for itself: "I have listened to the humans who cross my root bridges over the river in Lorraine. They have many of what you call emotions, some dualistic and some not: love and hate, jealousy and contentment, but others: fear, greed, sympathy, and I suppose there are many more I have not a word for yet. But I have feelings, compassion perhaps, but little of the other emotions. What do you make of this, Andy Mars?"

Andy did not know how to answer. "You have none of these feelings? You are neither happy or sad but at an equilibrium?"

"Perhaps."

Andy wondered if the Great Root knew the concept of being bored, but he did not ask that question.

Finally Andy felt mentally exhausted by the conversational ideas and decided he would try to talk to the river lizards more at another time. He said goodbye, but asked and received permission to bring Myra here. He wanted to share this experience with his great love and see what she thought.

*   *   *

The next day Andy brought Myra with him, explaining what was happening. Myra wanted to believe him, but she was almost ready to doubt Andy's sanity. Myra finally expressed herself strongly: "This sounds like a hallucinatory experience, as with some of the drugs."

"No, this is not like that. Just try."

They walked easily from the bridge down to the river and beyond. Andy wanted to try something else. They moved beyond where the Great Root was, to a place where only river lizards were lying on the bank.

"Now you must close your eyes and open your mind, and wait."

Myra smiled, as Andy had done the day before, but she complied and nodded. When the sensation swept them both she was astonished. Soon they were basking in the contentment of the river lizards. Andy felt he could spend all day every day here. It was so peaceful, such a happy conversation. The words wafted to them were witty, joking, a whole range of thoughts full of happiness, or what the river lizards expressed as "the good." There was such timeless peace, such a feeling of euphoria, like a return to childhood where time stretches out endlessly. In the end they had to shake loose, almost for fear of being trapped in a web of complacency that made leaving impossible.

When they did go, Myra said: "Andy I am leaving feeling many things. I do not know if I will ever understand their concept of 'the good,' but also there is some danger here, things not being disclosed, information held back, and as I feel with the Great Root, uncertainty. There is much more here if we could dig it out, but always as I approached the high truth in our conversation I was shunted off."

Was Myra hearing different things than he was, Andy wondered? Then Myra added: "Nothing must ever be allowed to happen to these wonderful creatures. Only Andy, as I said, there is some great mystery here too. They are not telling all they know."

"Like Myra?" Andy asked.

Myra flushed from her slender neck to her high cheeks. There was no answer, yet, no explanation of her personal mystery.

10

THE SECRET OF THE WOMAN OF THE RING

Then the day of the high adventure truly began. Captain Harley James and his space freighter returned for the monthly trading stop at Eden and delivered, along with the other interplanetary mail, a gold colored envelope with the seal and crest of the Emperor's Court. It was addressed to Andy Mars.

Andy was always in Lorraine to meet the space trader. He opened the letter in the spaceport restaurant where he had been awaiting Captain James arrival. That was the problem with being a success, Andy thought. You called attention to yourself. Soon the Empire would come with its ships. Steps needed to be taken, perhaps faster than he could act.

The letter was a personal summons to the Imperial Court of Justice, to explain the price of the Chalda Pills. He was given eleven standard days to appear and answer. It was simple, but might be a trap. The eleven days were just the time that it would take Captain James to arrive at Dethilm, the capital of the Empire. The letter promised safe passage and return, but that too might be a trap.

Andy showed the letter to the Captain who was sitting opposite him. Harley James nodded. "I hear that on some of the free planets they are pasting their own label over yours on the Chalda Capsules. The price is going up. It is a way with prices. People want more profit."

"Yet it may be a trap."

Harley James nodded. "It looks like you will be a passenger on my starship or become a fugitive or ..."

Andy nodded in turn. There were other possibilities here as well. "When do we leave?"

"Tomorrow noon. Be ready by nine. If all goes well we will board then or ..."

*   *   *

Andy Mars returned to his home to pack, think, and talk to Myra. Before he left he needed to speak to the Great Root as well and tell what everyone called "The Plant God" his situation.

And then Myra took Andy aside, away from Felicity and Happy, to her bedroom, their bedroom. She sat in the one of the two big armchairs facing the wide windows that looked out on the deck and garden. She motioned for Andy to sit opposite her. He expected she would be troubled, but there was more. Much more. Too much more. This did not bode well. It was time for true confessions.

"Andy," she began, "it is time I told you all about me. I have kept secrets from you that may prove disastrous. I feel you are going off to your death at the center of the Empire, and it is time I told you the truth. Then you can do with me what you will."

Andy felt tense. If Myra was not as she seemed, was anyone what they pretended to be? Was the whole world amiss?

*   *   *

Andy thought back to his first meeting Myra in the spaceport. He felt it was the most important day in his life. As far as Andy was concerned he and Myra enjoyed a great love. Is there anything better than young-love, the bonding that makes one a part of the sky, the stars, the whole universe? He had this strong, overwhelming feeling that he had not lived at all until that moment. The world was starting afresh.

One meets people and forms one impression of them, and then falls deeply in love and the impression becomes quite different.

He could forget everything with a love such as this. It was destiny; this height of passion, emotion, happiness.

Later, before they joined the Pilgrims on the Ark, they spent two weeks in a suite on the luxurious Space Resort on Belleine. They lay on the beaches, sat at the restaurants, danced at the nightclubs and especially spent days naked in the luxurious electronic beds, exploring the numerous stimulations available.

They indulged in all the absurdly beautiful conversation of love. Andy had looked at Myra and said: "You are my ideal of a sexy woman?" The words were too simple.

And she replied: "Don't you know Andy that you alone give me the power to be a sexy woman? It's all in your mind! It all emanates from you. I am a mere mirror, a reflection of your desire, a wish to make myself much more perfect than I can ever be."

"Perhaps, fair maiden," he answered archaically, "but methinks I have looked into other female mirrors and not had offered back such a fair reflection of my thoughts."

"So I will become your galactic tour guide." She kissed him. "We will go where you say and do as you wish. And I will tell you all about the galaxy."

"Have you been a tour guide for others?" He had to ask.

She laughed her lilting tinkle of happiness. "I have had a past life before I met you. I have looked upon other boys and later men and compared. But never before, Andy Mars, did I feel I would do whatever someone asked of me and only hoped they would ask much."

"What can I reply to that?"

Myra brushed her hair back in one of her typical flirting gestures. "You have made a conquest. Make the most of it. I am all yours to do with as you will." She leaned forward, waiting to be kissed.

They clung to each other then, naked, yet trying to get closer. Andy felt actually dizzy: "I want to extend this moment in time, to make it endless, to savor it forever, to hold it and to hold you." Are all men in love poets in their own mind? Yes, he wanted especially just now to find "forever."

But Myra too had responded in kind: "Andy, I love you. I keep having the same soft-frightened wish, over and over, that this will be a forever moment. It is a wild song I sing, disclosing feelings like stars merging. It is a chorus, a circus, fireworks, and lightning, deliberately making no sense. I am crazy about you. There is nothing I would not do for you." She placed herself on the line, as if on a wager, vulnerable, willing, surrendering, and supplicating. Every woman has that look she reserves for the man she really loves.

There was all the silly, important, banter that was love. Love does make fools of all men. "I'm most alive when I'm with you," Andy declared.

"I'm only alive when I'm with you," she replied.

"You taste so good. I could eat you whole."

"Where would you start?

"Both ends, your nose and your toes."

"But could you stomach the middle?"

"With you every night is New Year's Eve."

"What does it feel like when I kiss you like this?"

"Like I have the whole galaxy by the tail, like I'm on the edge of a great discovery."

And he told her: "I want to know all about you, the dolls you played with, the games you enjoy, the tears, the fears, the joys, the boys." Myra had told him much. But she always stopped short somehow. Would Andy feel he had been sleeping with the enemy? No, she could not spoil this wild, impossible dream with truth. Not now. But the longer truth was postponed, the harder it was to say the beginning words that would lead to disaster.

So what was the mystery now, yet to come that could nullify all else? Andy wondered and waited. Myra had avoided and gone around the central problem of her being. She had never mentioned the greatest mystery of her life. She had lied. "I was poor, and I ran away. I do not want to talk about it." This was all she said.

* * *

So now, four years later, Andy and Myra sat opposite each other in their bedroom in the city of Lorraine on Eden. There was a long silence. "So speak. It will be good to have the hidden secret of Myra at last revealed."

"Yes, my name is Myra. My last name on the Galactic passport is not true, and there is nothing else true about me."

Andy held back. "Go on."

"You know it's good to relocate, but its best to remember you bring the same problems and same person and same way of doing things to each new locale. There is something I must tell you, before you leave for your death in the center of the Empire."

She paused. "It is my terrible secret, which if ever discovered could make it worse for you. But perhaps they want me back. Perhaps you can use me as a trading chip. I will give up my life for you gladly, Andy." She extended a hand.

"What is it Myra? Some crime you have committed? Tell me then." Andy gripped her hand but he felt a terrible pain in his stomach, as he waited.

"It is worse than a crime. I am the enemy Andy. I fled the Empire. I am a daughter of the Emperor, Alexius V. I am a Princess of the realm." She took a deep breath and went on. "Sure, there are over two hundred Princesses, and this is of the inner conclave alone, and counting, but the Emperor holds tight to all his possessions. I was to be married to the ruler of Xantha, one of the Free Planets. It was a way to establish control for the Emperor. I was part of a bargain, a contract signed, a diplomatic game that was being played. His name is Selwin the Illustrious. He is an old man."

"You are a Princess?" Andy could hardly believe it. He was trying not to show too much emotion. It was too ludicrous. "There are disposable wives and children in the Empire" Andy added.

"So I fled," Myra continued. "But I also took money from the royal treasury before I departed. Money that was not mine. Money now spent. I represent all you and those on the Free Planets hate most, the Emperor and the Imperial Court."

"Is that all?" Andy leaned forward to hold her face between his hands for a moment, perhaps making it all the more difficult for Myra to go on.

"No. That was only a preamble, to avoid saying what I must say."

She was serious, and a tear left the corner of her eye and rolled along her nose. "Go ahead," Andy requested.

"One is born into a family relationship, Andy. There was my mother. That is a painful story and I will tell it to you soon. But first me. First my story. All families have a wisdom of their own. All have a way of being. Every one of us was once a child. We were all children, though we try to pretend we were not. Each child sees the world through the family they are born into and believes all the rest of the universe is like her own family. Sure other people dress differently and have other customs. But the child sees her family as the norm, the way things are. Later the child finds there are different ways of living, and if the child is clever, she may compare." Myra paused, looking at Andy.

Myra continued: "You accept the world around you as normal when you are a child. No one talks against it. In our case no one dared talk against it. Only after you are grown do you look back, examine, and consider. And then it is only some who presume to do that. Only the situation at court was more extreme."

"Well your father had you suckered in. He made you believe in his ways. Tell me about your life at court, Myra."

She almost straightened up. "I am a princess of the royal house of Nelob. I was a protected one. On Nelob I had attendants, serfs, and slaves." Then she laughed at herself, almost hysterically.

"Is this a declining hierarchy? What were the differences?"

Myra paused again, "No. Andy, you tell me again about your family. Why did you leave Earth?"

Andy shifted in his seat. It was a digression to give Myra time to think, perhaps. "My story is not as interesting as yours and you have heard most of it already. My family were well to do. Certainly not royalty. They lived on Oceania Four, one of the enormous man-made Pacific Islands. It was force screen enclosed to keep out the storms. Soil had been brought in. My family was old-wealth, but my father was an oddity, a second son. There were so few second children among the elite."

Andy paused: "I, of course, was an only child, as usual on Earth. We had a huge computerized farm on Oceania Four. This led to my early interest in the Agra Business. I was fascinated by the concept of how much could be grown to feed the world.

That was my childhood. I left to go to the University. Then I went off to advanced study on Mars. Talk about being out of touch. My father died in an accident and I could not even return for the funeral. My mother continued to manage what was a cooperative farm. While I was close to my mother, after I was unjustly accused and fled Mars, I was afraid to contact my mother again. The Empire reaches out secretly even on Earth."

Andy reflected: Perhaps he had been a radical, a secret rebel even then as a child. His mother had declared him so over minor offenses such as leaving food uneaten on his ever-clean plate or hunks of meat, which as a test, he speared on his ever-clean fork. His mother still had to tidy up after him.

Andy paused and then continued. "Yes," he admitted. "I have always hated the Empire. But now, more interestingly, let us get back to your story. Tell me instead, does your father, the Emperor Alexius V, really have two thousand wives as they say? What could anyone do with two thousand wives?"

"Are you jealous that you only have three?" Myra squeezed his hand. "I have never objected to your other two wives."

Maybe her upbringing had led Myra to accept the other two wives the Pilgrims had given to him.

"But I spend most of my time with you," Andy offered. Why was he on the defensive? He thought about this and began to feel anger.

"I appreciated being your favorite wife."

Was she serious, Andy wondered?

"It was difficult for me to believe when I first met you that you wanted me just for myself. I was one of so many in the palace on Dethilm."

"You are the most beautiful woman I ever met?" Andy replied simply.

"That is the correct answer." She laughed. "It is what we women all want to hear."

"But you did not answer my question. What could even the Emperor Alexius V do with two thousand wives?"

"What do you do with them? Well you have sex. You make babies."

"Yes, reputedly he has thousands of children. But two thousand wives!"

"Well it didn't start out with two thousand."

"There were mass marriages."

"Yes, that's true."

"But why two thousand? How many days in a Nelob year?"

"Less than Earth standard. And Earth has become the measure for all planets. There are about three hundred and ten days in a Nelob year. The orbit is not fixed. It varies. The planet wobbles and is unstable." Myra shifted in her chair uncomfortably. This conversation was taking an unexpected turn.

"So what were the sleeping arrangements?"

"I was not privy to all that went on. There were whispers. There were rumors. There was gossip. Some was no doubt untrue."

"With that many women and attendants there would be that."

"All right. Supposedly he slept with a new woman each night for the first years. His doctors determined the most fertile time for his wives. Then he slept with them. Only one out of three became impregnated. He had about a hundred children born in the normal way each year. He divided the women into three groups, the fertile, those who were pleasing and with whom he would try again, and the barren."

"Not much of a chance for the barren."

"Oh no. He was kind. The barren were given three chances over the years when they were most fertile. Later when the Emperor began the artificial insemination the barren women had even more opportunities. But these were the scientific children. Not of the first rank."

"What was your rank?"

Myra shook her head in disbelief at this question. "Yes, I was first rank with Honors. My mother was of the First Conclave. I was therefore one of the anointed."

"And yet you fled."

"Fled?" She laughed. "Yes. I ran. I deserted. I left in disguise. I stole from the royal treasury. Then I stole a royal space yacht. I wanted to see the universe and was not allowed to travel. I was not even allowed to leave the palace. This was a triple crime. And after I fled, the first thing that happened when I got far off planet, after some jumps in hyper-space, I was hit by space pirates, who took the yacht."

Myra took a deep breath and went on: "It was very scary. They almost had me too. I had spotted a habitable planet I was considering when they hit me. I blasted out into space in a suit. I took the money and little else. They looked for me and no doubt would have held me for ransom. Or worse. Anyway, once I had blasted clear, it was hard for them to find me, to locate a lone person drifting in space. I decided I would just die in space when the air ran out. Then I managed to reach the habitable planet before the air ran out in the tank. I slowed my descent with the thruster boots. I was extremely lucky. When I landed I booked passage out, and began traveling by passenger star ship. I paid to procure false identity, keeping my first name. Later I met you, Andy Mars."

"They call themselves privateers," Andy agreed. "But you are right, they really are space pirates. They have powerful ships that can outrun most of the Emperor's battleships. But they don't fight the Empire. They attack merchant ships and passenger ships. They run from what they can't fight and are the bane of the Empire. I ran into them twice as a captain of a star ship. Once I outmaneuvered them and the second time got in a lucky blast first. But, let's keep to the subject. Your father did it with three hundred and ten women the first year of his reign?"

"More like three hundred. There were days off. There were also favorite wives who entertained him. My mother was one of the inner conclave, as I said, and a favorite."

"Hooray. So a hundred got pregnant each year?"

"Yes. They had two years off to raise the child before he tried again."

"So they were replaced by a hundred others. You don't need more than four hundred or five hundred wives in that case.

If he was in operation three hundred days a year and added one hundred more each year and then returned to the original. What of the barren wives?"

"Some of them were artificially inseminated later. They were the second conclave, the outer ones, the lessor wives. But they never attained the royal bed again."

"I still don't understand. Why two thousand? And the failures were never his fault, huh?"

Myra laughed. "I was not present for the attempts. Some he eliminated on sight and picked another for the night. Or they were turned away after he talked to them."

"That's the trouble with mass marriages," Andy observed. "You never do get to know them. Then he talked as well as had sex?"

Myra straightened and stiffened. The whole situation was worse even than she had imagined in a hundred thoughts about how this might all be told. "This is horrible," Myra complained. "You are going off to your death and I am trying to confess and all you want is information and to embarrass me. I love only you. You are the air I breathe."

"I love you too. But why two thousand wives? I really want to know."

"That number is all you come back to. I have no answer. Some were not congenial. Some were barren. Others produced children every two years as my mother did. From age sixteen to forty-five years my mother had fifteen children. She was one that was of the inner conclave with honors, a favorite."

"How about those wives treated with the fertility drugs who had three or four or five of the Emperor's children each year? Twins, triplets, and quads? I have heard those stories?"

"They were the failures in a way, experimented upon. Some did have forty or fifty children. One wife had sixty-two children. She had a lot of twins and sets of triplets. She held the record. But those who were not naturally implanted by the Emperor in person were looked upon as sports, oddities, experiments by the others of the court."

"The artificial insemination started later then?"

"Yes."

Andy paused, thinking. He could hardly believe it. He tried to take it all in. His Myra! "You are a princess of the royal family," he finally blurted out, repeating, really astounded. "You have the royal blood to marry into one of the other planetary rulers and be part of the whole royal orbit." "The Emperor liked to have trusted members of his family marry into other large kingdoms, so that there was a relationship of blood as well as power to bind the planets. I could only be a Queen in someone else's domain. It was not what I wanted."

Then Myra paused and scoffed, "royal blood! How far back does my father's line go? The royal blood phrase is much bandied about in court. My father! The historians are busy now altering the history of his family. Four generations now." Myra thought of all she was saying. Would what she was saying do any good at all? Would Andy Mars still love her when she had talked herself empty and told the final big secret?

Myra continued: "The Emperor, my father, his great grandfather rose by killing many people and seizing a country. His grandfather turned the country into planetary control and began to expand. His father became an emperor of many star systems. My father has expanded the empire enormously. What is royal about that? All men have the blood of slaves and thieves in them from the deep past. Did I want to be a pawn in this galactic chess game? No, I much preferred trying to make my own life, my own decisions, my own mistakes, traveling my own route, and especially having my own man." She touched Andy with her hand as no other woman could.

"If that was the genealogy, why was he Alexius V?"

"At court you dared not say that. He has made his family of rulers older than it is. He is absurdly enamored by the trappings of royalty."

Then Andy looked into Myra's pretty face, down into her wide liquid blue eyes, an ocean one could drown in, and holding her narrow shoulders in his large hands he spoke seriously. "I want the direct and honest truth now."

"I have never told you indirect or dishonest truths."

"Perhaps because I did not ask the right questions." He squeezed a little on her precious face.

"Andy I am going to tell you some truths that are not found in the books on Fam-Soc."

"You are saying many words and pretending they are wisdom, Myra. Do you have a point in all this?" Andy Mars replied. "So you had everything, as a spoiled poor, little rich girl, and it was not enough."

"My mother had everything too." Myra laughed. "You have not heard it all. This is the part that is most difficult to tell. It sets my siblings and me apart. My mother was the woman who bargained. She wanted to be special, set apart. She was the woman who had her demands placed in the wedding contract. She was the woman of the diamond."

Andy's eyes widened in spite of himself. "I have heard the rumors, the stories about that. It is true, then?"

"Yes, sad but true. Most women dared not bargain. There is an old saying that the worst thing is to get what you want."

"Your mother was greedy. I hate to say it."

"It proved her undoing. She demanded the largest diamond possible for her wedding ring. She wanted something apart from the other wives. She wanted possessions. She demanded the largest diamond ring ever bestowed. They were fabricating diamonds on the free planets, but my mother would have none of it." Myra paused.

"My mother's diamond weighed two hundred pounds by the old measure, eighty kilos, and after the ceremony, after the wedding night, it was attached to her finger by a ring with a lock only the Emperor could remove. The Emperor had abided by the contract and it became a great joke at court."

"Not carats?' Andy asking, smiling.

"No. A carat is a mere two hundred milligrams. We all came to know this only too well. My father gave her a diamond from Grando-Sierra. It was imbedded at the bottom in a silver support. The ring was locked over my mother's finger. Four eunuchs carried the diamond on a pillow to the high cathedral for the wedding ceremony. Then they returned my mother to her bridal bedroom. My father had kept his promise. But my mother could never leave her bedroom again. She was locked to her treasure forever."

"That was your mother! Well, she got what she asked for. I have heard that story. It is hard to believe. It is told as just a wild tale of the Emperor's court."

"She had a personal, private bedroom, unlike many of the other wives, but she never left it again. She was the prisoner of the ring. The Emperor had the only key to the ring. She certainly encouraged his occasional visits and her temporary release. I was the first born. At the time my father was starting out. He had less than two hundred wives."

"A mere pittance."

"All things have a value depending upon their scarcity. When the rich diamond fields were uncovered in Grando-Sierra, natural diamonds could become as common as any other rocks. When the Emperor took control of Grando-Sierra, no more diamonds were exported than were necessary so as to keep the price in place. My mother was greedy and my father thought it was a very funny joke."

Andy reflected. "The diamond cartels established trading restrictions on old Earth in early times to keep the prices up also. It was a created scarcity. So you grew up in a strange family. But how did you feel about your father? It must have been hard to dislike him."

"I have been waiting for you to change, Andy Mars."

"You think I will give you a ring that will be your prison?"

"No. But leaders become powerful because of their personalities. They can't avoid their charisma. The great leaders want more and more power. The circle is vicious as leadership creates more power and power greater leadership."

"'All power corrupts. Absolute power corrupts absolutely.' Lord Action, an early Earth historian said that. But if the problem is recognized, perhaps it can be avoided."

Myra laughed sadly. "The Emperor Alexius V had many jokes. He changed his wives names to please himself. He gave them new official names. There were flavors such as Ginger. He said Ginger could snap. And Joy. He said he often jumped for Joy. It was carried too far. There were wives he named after flowers such as Daisy, Pansy, Magnolia, Iris, Violet, Dahlia, Heather, Lily, Lilac, Rose and oh so many of them. My father said he liked to pull their petals."

Myra sighed now: "Of course the Pilgrim women have odd names, only this was different. There were other fanciful names for the palace queens. I remember Cookie and Crystal, and Fancy. Sometimes he liked rhymes. He gave twin wives the names Candi and Dandi. There were girls named after fruits: Cherri, Peaches, Tangerine. There were bird names: Swallow, Lark, Warbler. Oh, there were many more."

"The Emperor's new wives." It was as a take-off on the old story. Andy shook his head. "Your mother was the woman of the ring." This was hard to believe.

"Yes. At least I always knew where my mother was. The story of the woman of the ring has spread throughout the planets."

"So who watched all these women?"

"The palace is run by thousands of clones. Each set of servants was created for a special purpose. They were eunuchs. There are robot cleaners of course, but cloned humans were cheaper and looked more suitable. We called them drones. Of course among the women and children there was much gossip about what others were doing and who the current favorites were. There was much backstabbing. People usually talk about people rather than ideas, unfortunately."

"So what was it like growing up in a harem?" Andy asked. "Harem scarum."

"The children hung out together naturally. They exchanged information. The schools in the palace for the children were sexually segregated. My father did not want the half brothers and sisters to get into trouble with each other."

"Incest begins at home," Andy interjected, laughing.

"That was the big taboo," Myra went on doggedly with a straight face. "The only males I saw were my half-brothers, the eunuchs, and the clones. Many of the children had a fear of the outside, of traveling, of leaving the palace because we were taught it was safe there. It was really a phobia for some. It bordered on perversion."

"What is perverse?" Andy asked. "What is normal? It seems to me that with two thousand wives and thousands of children, there could be no normal."

"I recognized I was being programmed," Myra replied simply. "The women were taught to find the right man and then surrender to him completely. Finding the right man is harder than surrendering. We girls talked and joked about having to kiss a lot of frogs in order to find the fairy story prince. We all, the Emperor's daughters and sons alike, felt we were in a gigantic orphanage with mothers but no real father. No father could have individual time for thousands of children. A father is a king in his home, perhaps. Maybe he goes to work all day. But a good father comes home sometimes."

"And your father? How did he have an effect? How did he exert paternal influence with that many children?"

"My father must be careful. There is Justin, the oldest born boy, who is being groomed to be Alexius VI. He will have to change his name. But my father fears regicide. Not by Justin, but perhaps by some other son. Many are now adults."

"It is a problem of having hundreds of sons," Andy agreed. "The father of Alexius V sterilized all but one son according to the stories." Andy quoted the secret but well known history of the Empire. "Still your father took the throne by killing his own father and then all his brothers and sisters. 'People live too long,' your father is reported as saying when he committed patricide. He was tired of waiting. But how do you raise a family of thousands of wives and thousands of children with murder as a family background? Can he not see what will happen at his death? There will be a terrible massacre of the children by whoever acquires the throne."

"The problems of power," Myra agreed. "And sometimes there has been an argument among the children that has led to violence. There have been several royal murders within the palace already, always investigated, but the guilty not always found. Still my father has been ruler now for almost thirty years."

"Walking around with a personal force screen," Andy added. Myra did not reply to this but concluded instead: "When the Space Pirates attacked my yacht I sent out a distress signal.

Later when I was reached safety anyway I regretted sending this signal and calling attention to myself. My hope now is that my father and his spies think I am captured or dead and are not still looking for me."

Andy felt first shocked and now somehow betrayed by Myra's tale. "Why did you not trust me enough to tell this story before?"

"When I first met you, you told me how the soldiers of the Empire had unfairly come after you. How you had to flee the University on Mars. You hated the Empire and my father, the Emperor and all he represented. That is a widespread feeling on the Free Planets. I did not tell you at first, and then I could not."

Andy now reflected that it was also a well known fact that the Emperor had agents and spies on all the planets. One must assume these agents also existed on Eden. They were sleeper moles, going about their business, but infiltrated into the society, reporting back, maybe staying a lifetime and never being noticed if there was no need for their information. Now that Eden had money flowing in from the sale of the Chalda Elixir, the reports of a spy increased in value. There had to be such spies among the Pilgrims or in Lorraine the capital of Eden. Myra could even be such a one. No. Andy dismissed this idea. He was becoming too suspicious. Andy was not worth sending out a daughter of the Emperor before the Chalda Elixir was discovered and successful. But now with the Chalda so valuable, there certainly were spies, old or now.

Again Andy inquired: "What is the palace like? Is it as splendid as they say?"

Myra shrugged. "The palace stands fifty stories high. It was modeled on Versailles in old France before the Earth's Nuclear Wars. But Versailles was built before force screen lift elevators. It is the most expansive, most expensive palace ever built. Six thousand rooms. Home!" She laughed. "It has these huge open spaces, twenty, thirty, and fifty stories high, with waterfalls and greenery everywhere. Much of the interior is like a great garden. Actually the main problem I have with Eden is that it is so much like home. No one knows what one of the wonders of ancient Earth, the hanging gardens of Babylon, really looked like. But the palace has hanging gardens. Inside the atrium the plants with flowers grew suspended from invisible points on a force screen, cascading trellises of beauty."

Andy was looking at Myra closely now, and he decided suddenly he wanted to examine all of her parts, so as not to forget anything, in case he was locked up in some cell forever by the Emperor.

11

THE SUMMONS TO THE EMPIRE

Before he left for the capital of the Empire, Andy Mars had just time to wander down to the bridge near the capital at Lorraine and have another conversation with the Great Root. "It is time I carried out the rest of my bargain," he declared. "You asked me to spread some of your seeds on another world and I shall try to do so. I can't think of a more interesting place than the capital of the Empire."

The words from the Root came into his mind: "This should not be the end of our relationship."

"No," Andy replied aloud. "Not at all. If I live through my present journey, that is. But it fulfills the promise I made."

"I see in your mind you believe you have done much for me. That is fitting that you should do much, since humans are the newcomers. But there are still things we can do for each other."

"Well, I have been guaranteed safe passage, but I hope that I am allowed to return to Eden?"

"You do not trust the Emperor?" came the words in his head from the Root. It was becoming easier to understand these words with practice.

"No." And Andy related his feelings about the Empire once again. Did the Great Root and the river lizards alike, long-lived species, find Andy Mars abrupt. Humans had to hurry. What was time to a plant?

"How big are your seeds?" Andy asked, again feeling abrupt.

"You will find one type of my spore on the yellow flowers along the edge of the road. They are not air plants; they are me. As with so many plants on this planet, I have caused these to grow to human specifications of beauty."

Andy had seen the same flowers on many a table. What was a plant's conception of beauty? Did a flower give a silent scream when it was cut? "Will the seeds all be fertile?" Andy inquired. "What percentage will germinate?" He did not wish to have to do the job twice.

"Yes. Most will be. Nature is prolific and redundant. Not all the seeds will survive, depending upon where they are planted."

"Do you have planting instructions?"

"Soil, water, sunlight. A garden of small flowers is ideal."

"I may not be able to do more than scatter these upon the garden. To dig and plant on a strange planet could cause attention."

"With enough seeds, even a scattering should be successful."

"But if your flowers look different than the garden, they may be plucked and destroyed."

"You forget, I can mimic."

"And defend yourself?" Andy asked.

"True. What is your plan?" the Great Root inquired.

"I can sense a further symbiotic relationship in the making."

"I am not sure," Andy advised. "On what sort of other planets would like your progeny scattered?"

"You are exporting a plant elixir from this planet already, the Chalda capsules." The Root was so often indirect.

"That is true. But that is not seeds."

"If I were unscrupulous, it could be," the Great Root confided.

"What do you mean?" Andy had a sudden cold fear.

"Anything can be seeds. Cuttings. Fruit. Berries. Ingested and then excreted. The fact that I am telling you this, should show what you call morality. Morality prevents good men from stealing without thinking of punishment in a Pilgrim hereafter. They do right for the sake of the right itself. The highest morality is doing right, not from fear of being caught or later punishment, but for the sake of right as a concept. It is philosophy that I heard from the river lizards and I agree. I can mimic other plants. I can slide my roots underground and attach myself to the roots of other plants. I could take over the Chalda and produce a drug that made all men who took it my slaves. The capsules could be liquid seeds as well. Now I sense that I have frightened you, Andy Mars. That was not my intention. I was trying to reassure you. To answer your question, you are an exporter of plants already with the Chalda Capsules. Are there planets that export plants or their seeds to other worlds?"

"You wish to be sent to grow where you can mimic plants that will be exported throughout the galaxy as far as humans roam?"

"Exactly."

"That is more than saving my life is worth, perhaps. I should instead declare this planet off limits, cause the humans to leave, and destroy it. Again, I am speaking directly as you did. My first interest must not be to myself, but to humanity, for I am involved in all of mankind."

"Well said. But I intend to live in a symbiotic relationship with all humans."

"And all life?" Andy asked.

"Yes, I see what you mean. Mimicking and destroying other plants could cause us to be left with men, animals, and myself. No, I have long lived in harmony with the other plants on this planet, even after I achieved primacy. I could have destroyed all other plants and did not. If I had destroyed wantonly there would have been no Chalda Thorns. I shall not change my ways on other planets."

"But how do I know, oh brother, oh Great Root who saved my life, that perhaps you saved me for a purpose. Perhaps you are already all the plants on this planet: the Chalda Thorn, the pastures of grass, the flowers, the trees, the bushes, the food men eat, the weeds we pluck, the vines and the jungle in all its tangle?"

There was a long pause. "You could run tests. But you do not know how. You wish to trust and you will have to. The Pilgrims have what they call Faith, a belief that transcends logic."

"There is one city and one planet where I might especially welcome changes," Andy declared.

"And that is?"

"Dethilm, the capital city on Nelob the central planet of the Empire."

"Then take me there."

"Yes. I will. But Dethilm is not empty land, jungle and farm, pasture and prairie, with scant human population as Eden. It is a massive urban planet devoted to technology and the population is large, for slave labor has been forcibly imported and sometimes even created as clones, man-made slaves."

"Always things are to be seen in due course. And after a season I will need to be in touch with my offspring."

"I will be your intermediary, if I may and if I can."

"You are concerned about this Empire. Tell me more about it. I sense in you a reluctance to tell me about the evil men sometimes do. You have avoided such conversations before."

"Yes. But have you too conquered, Great Root? You speak of subsuming all others of your own kind, joining with them, but does that not mean control, domination? We are concerned as humans with death to the self."

"No. It was not like that. Our personalities merged, and sometimes still vary at a distance, but we have basic agreement."

"For your species. Well, let me tell you more of the Empire." And Andy Mars explained in some detail most of his problem.

After he finished the Great Root replied: "Very well. The adventure begins for us both. If the Empire destroys this planet, to get to you, Andy Mars, they will kill me as well. I do not fancy my kind will go on, in the human fashion without me. That is a problem with being one. We are together in this project. I have not taken sides in human affairs, except to help you as an individual survive, Andy Mars. Now I will have to take sides."

"The Empire does not want to destroy the Chalda. But I can see some ships coming to remove specimens of the Chalda Plant. That would be a first step. Once they successfully grow the Chalda elsewhere, this whole planet might be destroyed."

"I can see the problem. We will see, Andy Mars. They can remove Chalda plants, but they will not be successful in growing the Chalda elsewhere."

"Why not?"

"All in good time." There was more, but the Great Root evaded further questions. Andy took time to say goodbye to his plant friend.

Then he went to the suggested flowers and shook them gently. The small black seeds, no larger than pepper grains, fell into his hand. He was amazed again at the oddities of nature. Some small plants had quite large seeds and other huge trees had spoor that were the size of poppy seeds on a loaf of bread. The dozens of seeds he held in his hand were all together small enough to be concealed in a few of the Chalda capsules. Andy saw one solution even in this beginning. The problem of smuggling the seeds was solved in a moment.

* * *

Andy felt satisfied as to the conditions on Eden as he prepared to leave. John Kent, the former governor, was back managing things; he did say he enjoyed keeping a hand in the governing on occasion. Myra was overseeing the Chalda pill output on the planet. The long corridors of the new Chalda production factories buzzed with the activity of producing billions of pills a week.

Simon Semple asked to come along with Andy to Dethilm. He added he was worried about Andy, as his leader journeyed to the very capital of the Empire. "Many men flee when they receive the Emperor's summons," Simon observed.

"The Emperor's summons suggests nothing but that I make an appearance," Andy replied. "It promises safe passage and return."

"But men disappear," Simon declared.

* * *

The space flight itself was uneventful except for one incident. Two days out on the voyage Simon had gotten into a quarrel with a star freighter crewmember and they were preparing to fight it out with knives. Andy had intervened. It was a meaningless quarrel. It was one thing to kill for a reason, another to fight over mere words. Andy remembered Simon's pole fighting with Skip Boyton of the River Rats. Simon got into trouble too easily.

The star freighter was on its regular route, which touched on only one other port before Dethilm. Andy had done all this before as an officer on a star freighter, and later as a navigator of the galaxy. There were two days flying at full speed until they were out far enough for the hyperdrive to be safely kicked in. Then two days of maneuvering inward to another planet's dock. A day of unloading cargo followed and then the same procedure continued in the flight to the Imperial capital, Dethilm.

Here, as they approached the Empire's Center, there was a star fighter ship escort into the global space lock. Ships were lined up here, floating, waiting their turn to enter. There was only one way onto the planet. Dethilm had a force screen clear around it, extending out fifty kilometers. There was one space lock that opened for star ships coming in and another for star ships that were leaving. The star freighter commanded by Captain Harley James, that Andy Mars was on, sat in the space lock in quarantine until the ship and passengers were examined.

Dethilm custom's officers in their blue uniforms and epaulets boarded the star freighter. Give a man a fancy uniform and he becomes important. They checked for weapons and bombs. After the cargo and the ship itself were inspected, the passengers and crew were lined up and examined. Simon was carrying a weapon and it was confiscated. Andy Mars was carrying Chalda Pills, as were many of the passengers. The pills were examined, but not opened. They were no novelty to the customs agents.

The star freighter was now free to move through the force lock and dock. Force field unloading began. Andy had done it before, but it was always interesting to step off a thousand meters above the ground and find the nothingness that was solid, carrying you down as an elevator might.

On the ground, as they passed through final inspection beams, there was an enormous shock for Andy Mars. On the bulletin board all newcomers had to pass by, there were pictures of those wanted for questioning by the Empire. But one picture stood out. The words in the universal language under it offered: "Have you seen this woman? One million credits reward. Inform the guards." The picture was that of Myra!

Andy looked and then looked again. There was no doubt it was Myra. He next shifted to Simon, who also was looking and then glancing away.

Simon had not seen Myra that much, for she kept out of sight as much as possible in town. But now Simon probably knew.

Andy excused himself and had a quick private conversation with a blue-uniformed guard. "Who is the woman who is wanted?" Andy inquired of the guard?"

"Do you have information?"

"No. But why is she so singled out with such a large reward? You must be looking for many people?"

"True, we are. There are whole computers full of names, pictures, and retina scans. Perhaps you are one. She is one of the Emperor's family. She ran off or was kidnapped. I know nothing more."

The long line wound by the high machines. Each person went up for the eye scan. Then they advanced to the final inspection desk.

The guard looked up at Andy Mars. "You are summoned for questioning by the High Imperial Court. Your appearance is due tomorrow afternoon at two o'clock our local time. Be early. You are also wanted for questioning on Mars in a radical conspiracy. But that was a long time ago and is not now the affair of the Empire's." Still they remembered or had records.

Simon was passed with a nod. The two stayed in line, proceeding through a great hall and then out onto the street. Andy waited till they were alone to ask: "Why were you passed by so easily? There should be a record of former soldiers of the Empire. You told me you left your post."

"All is not perfect in the Empire, Andy. There are ways to bribe and destroy records. When I left my post I did not want a record. I gave myself an honorable discharge."

They checked into a hotel at the port. Andy had one morning to inspect the planet before his court appearance. He told Simon he wished to walk around alone.

"You'll need me," Simon grunted.

"I just wish to explore, and I wish to do it alone." Suddenly Andy was not certain of Simon and besides he was wondering if his companion was suicidal after the fight he had nearly gotten into on the star freighter.

*   *   *

Dethilm was a huge city, spread out, but with great towering buildings also. These structures were not so visible at ground level. At one end of the city in a great central square was the tallest building ever constructed, three thousand meters high, more for show, to make a point about the power of the Empire. But Andy was more interested in the palace, at the other end of the city. He inquired and took the moving pedways to the area of the palace.

The Emperor's palace and gardens had their own private force shield around them, invisible, and here there was a shield within a shield within a shield, massive invisible technology. There was a force screen around the entire planet and then another around the capital city of Dethilm. Andy was within both of these screens at the moment. There was then a third force screen at the edge of the city encompassing the huge palace of the Emperor and its gardens. And these gardens had in turn a force screen around them.

If you wished to enter the city you had to pass through the force screen and submit to a full search by viewscreen. If you wished to enter the Emperor's garden on one of the open free days for a pleasant walk, you again were subject to a viewscreen. The palace beyond the gardens, with its separate force shield, no one entered unless summoned by the Emperor.

The gardens were about three kilometers wide and four kilometers long, with many kinds of flowers, shrubs, and trees.

Green meadows surrounded the force screen and gate enclosed gardens, so that visitors had to walk a kilometer to the gateway. Further down, two kilometers away, were a series of brightly-lit casinos.

Along the center of the garden pathway leading toward the palace were some magnificent Crescent Trees that had been imported from the planet Glander. These tall flowering trees bent in a crescent, and had their tops connected, one with the next, so that they presented a picture of a double row of flowering purple trees pointing right at the back palace gates. The road from the city to the palace led through the middle of the gardens and the Crescent Trees lined both sides.

The palace beyond was almost Byzantine in style with many towers and domes atop of domes. Andy could see the splendid palace structure, but the force screen precluded a visit.

Luckily the gardens were open to the public that morning and Andy Mars entered. He was aware of the viewscreens adroitly concealed in the bushes. There were a number of visitors including small children running about. Andy paused, at a drinking fountain, gently shaking into his hand the contents of seeds hidden in one Chalda pill. He pretended to consume the pill and in examining the flowers and hedge left a small trail of seeds along the Emperor's Garden beside the path.

The scattering of seeds seemed to be such a futile gesture, trivial, silly, yet he had tried. Now it was up to fate. He could not safely push the seeds into the ground or even water the seeds here in the garden

127

where he was being watched by so many surveillance screens. The seeds were on their own now and for better or worse had their only chance.

Andy noticed a few seeds still stuck to his palm. After leaving the garden and the surveillance, he shook these seeds into a broad lawn and bent to push two into the ground while tying his shoe. He had tried. It seemed so hopeless, no more than a shout into a high wind.

* * *

The High Court of Dethilm was supposedly aiming to establish universal law in the galaxy. There was a whole new law code, the Galactic Compendium that had recently been completed. The actual aim was to exert the Emperor's control everywhere. The court building itself was huge and the high court chambers were not one, but many enormous rooms, each producing a splendid effect with their real brown wood.

The court had assigned an attorney to Andy, and in the end it was apparently a simple matter. Or so it seemed. Andy was nervous and his balding, somber attorney was obviously a bureaucratic hack who would bend with any pressure and then collect his required fee from Andy. The courtroom was crowded with many people waiting for their moment of justice. They were called before the bench by their names appearing on a large screen.

The judge, dressed in traditional open sleeved black robes, sat up above at his bench with his computer. There were advisors on either side of the judge. Yet he was a youngish man for a judge, a callow faced functionary.

Andy appealed that he had correctly labeled the bottles of Chalda Pills and his profit was not large for each pill. It was of course the volume that made the difference.

"Why is the price so low, marked originally as one credit per capsule?"

Andy almost was tempted to say: "Are you upset with me for taking too little, for not overcharging?" Instead he spoke humbly, his head bowed down before the authority: "I wanted to make these beneficial pills available to as large a market as possible at a reasonable price. I did not want to deprive the poor of the Chalda pills advantages." He did not say that selling billions at a low unit cost still produced an enormous profit.

The Judge keyed in the computer for this case. "Do you realize the labels have been removed on some planets and the capsules are selling for five, ten, even twenty credits each?"

Andy was actually shocked. He said so.

"A decree will be entered that in any place the profit may not be over twenty percent on the Chalda Pills. There also shall be a twenty percent tax leveled by the Emperor. That notification must appear on the original bottle label. Also overlabeling or removal of the label will mean a sentence of death. Is that understood?"

"Yes, I agree. I shall see that the labels are changed. I can even produce bottles that will have the name and price embedded in the bottle, so that it can not be changed. But that will not stop people from putting another label over the bottle or taking the pills out and putting them in other bottles with other labels. Nor can I enforce the law."

The judge readily accepted that the oversight of the Emperor's law was necessary. The Empire was again entering into transactions to bring order, but also to control. It was swift decision with no appeal. Nor, Andy felt, was it really the judge's decision, but rather something decided in advance by the Emperor or his Council, entered into the computer, and all presented for the judge to act upon.

And the matter was not finished. The judge continued to consult the computer screen on this case and continued: "Now there is another matter. You will also present the formula for the Chalda Pills to the Imperial Chemistry Laboratories."

"That cannot be done," Andy declared. "There is no formula. It is a natural plant."

"Will you sell some of these plants to the Empire?" the Judge inquired blandly.

"They are risky to harvest. Many men have died of an overdose. They are indigenous to Eden and may not grow easily elsewhere."

"Answer the question. Will you sell some?"

"It is our chief export. We will not sell."

There was a pause and then the questioning changed again. "Why are you building many nuclear fission plants on Eden when it is a frontier planet?"

"We are using our profits for future power sources."

"Know this Andy Mars, the Chalda Pills will come under the Imperial Domain." No date was set for such a take-over but the threat was clearly spoken.

There was more, but it was toying; it was mere formality. He was free to leave. "You are here under the auspicious of safe passage by the Emperor's Court, and you may return to Eden on the next outbound ship. We will contact you further."

The matter was obviously not settled, but the judge had followed his instructions from the computer.

Andy thanked the judge and paid his required lawyer who had done nothing. He and Simon returned to their hotel. Apparently he had escaped some punishment for an unknown crime.

*   *   *

"I wish to further scout out this city of Dethilm and explore it, and this time you may come along," Andy invited.

Simon nodded. "You did not want me along this morning while you strolled in the palace garden and now I am welcome. I could observe in the courtroom from a distance, but was ordered not to speak. Now Andy Mars I will tell you what I think. Perhaps we should stay in the hotel tonight and go right out to the ship in the morning for the return trip to Eden. I do not like this planet. We were granted safe passage, and that included walking out of the court. Now we must get back safely to Eden. The Empire and the Emperor are not to be trusted."

"I hear you. But I would like to get the feel of this planet and especially its capital city. I would like to understand it better."

"In one evening?" Simon laughed. "The Imperial City of Dethilm is many things," Simon growled now. "I have been here before. If you want the real feel of an important part of this city it is not to be found in air scooter traffic, riding the created invisible lanes of the force field, but in one of the soldier's bars. They are dangerous, but offer many diversions.

If you really insist upon doing this, then let us try a soldier's bar if you want a little excitement."

"I do not want useless quarrels," Andy warned. "We will pick our enemies. So I ask you to be careful and circumspect."

"I shall be humble as the dust. I already apologized for what happened on the ship coming over here."

Andy nodded. They took a scooter taxi to another section of town. The scooters followed the high interior force screens on many levels above and around the buildings. The force field lanes were five levels high and six levels wide, all invisibly slotted in. The scooters were equipped with radar deflectors and there was no usual way the vehicles could get within three meters of each other. The scooters were very fast, but unless someone did something extraordinary, there were seldom accidents. It was Earthen technology, which was necessary on the overcrowded mother planet, but seemed a bit much for the Imperial City of Dethilm. Only, of course, as capital of the Empire, Dethilm was rich, and possessed everything it wanted. The Empire taxed everyone.

They arrived at the soldier bar. This establishment was named "Degradation" for no reason Andy saw as yet. The bar consisted of one enormous hall with a high vaulted ceiling. There were many patrons, largely military. Andy paused in the entranceway, trying to take it all in. There was singing and talk, a live band playing in the far background, and many side rooms some stretching out of sight behind pulled drapes. Andy and Simon sat in an alcove on the side, where they could observe. Simon ordered drinks, Kaputt, a strong frontier planet concoction. Obviously Simon had been here before.

The crowd was a mixture of soldiers, women, and some people of the city. The imperial soldiers wore their typical black uniforms, but no caps here. The Empire was a military state, but hid its power as much as possible. There were few galactic televised parades, little show of the great power. The full strength of the Empire's army was not to be found in books of statistics.

The soldiers in this bar talked openly of the star fighter shipbuilding programs on Dethilm and the opportunities that lay open to good men in the military. The Empire bought weapons from the Free Planets, but they were building their own secret weapons as well. It was the only way to achieve security.

There were intervals of rousing singing. The military songs were of conquest, of war, of adventure, of love of battle and spitting in the eye of death. There was much comradery. Two soldiers were talking about how to keep a flat down warbird flying after it hit an electronic screen.

One women got up nearby on one of the twenty-meter long tables filled with drinking soldiers and said loudly: "Everyone watch me."

A spotlight from above was suddenly directed on her. She was a little slim creature, young, with skin a little too unhealthy pale white and frazzled bright red hair. She was a bit shaky. Quickly she slipped off all her clothes, so they lay at her feet. Her face had the rosy flush of youth combined incongruously with the lines of age. Andy tried to guess her age. She was perhaps twenty, but she might have been five years younger or ten years older. She took her drink and swallowed it down at a gulp, shuttered all over for a moment and then as the band played trying to keep up, she began to move in a dance faster than any human could. She became a blur of activity. Her flesh almost seemed to leave her bones.

"She is drinking Pasquen," Simon declared.

"I have heard of this," Andy Mars replied. "But why does she do it?"

"She is addicted. It is already too late for her. Someone may have slipped her some once or she has a death wish. Now she needs a daily fix. It is thought a coup by some of the soldiers to slip this drug into a very young female's drink, to destroy as young a person as possible. She now feels life without her drug is useless. Do you know Andy what the half-life of this stuff is? Twenty to forty doses, one a day, and she will be dead, burned out. But if she stops she will die also. You use up your whole life in days. You do not eat nor want to."

The girl was moving so fast that it was impossible to follow the dance. The soldiers below and around her laughed, applauded, and urged her to go faster, but they also nudged each other knowingly.

"Are there no laws on the home planet of the Empire against this?" Andy inquired.

"The soldiers are allowed a certain latitude," Simon replied. "There is no major war right now. Aggressive spirits need entertainment."

They watched the girl dance. "We can not save her," Andy opined sadly. "But if this is what the Imperial soldiers are allowed to do for sport in the capital city of the Empire, this is one more reason to hate the Imperial power."

"She will drop exhausted after a bit and sleep until tomorrow night," Simon advised. "I always felt it would be amusing to have a woman like that and watch her burn up and die. But then the other side of me felt it was just too wicked to slip such a drug into a female's drink."

Then a little, dark man with the shiftiest eyes Andy had ever seen, a nervous creature, emerged like a blackbird from the shadows, glancing about and seeming ready to run at any moment. Yet he came over to their small table, nodded, and sat down without even being asked.

Andy examined the stranger who inquired furtively: "You are the Chalda King. You were at the High Court today. Will you sell some Chalda plants? Everything has its price."

"This is without price. Why do you think I would sell to you when I refused the high court of the Empire?"

"The Emperor will take what he wants, and perhaps there will be nothing left. Some of the Free Planets could start their own Chalda production, and then the Emperor would not be as interested in you as the technology spread. The sale to me could save your life."

"And you represent the Free Planets," Andy scoffed.

"I could."

"We all could represent anyone if we had something to sell. If the Association of Free Planets wishes to discuss this matter with me, they should send a delegation to Eden. If everyone had the Chalda, it would be worthless. You suggest that I destroy what I have by giving it to all. Then I would be safe. You would profit, and I would have little."

"Then you would be safe," the stranger repeated.

"Safe with nothing." Andy wondered why he was even talking to this man. But he was curious.

"I am more of an intermediary," the little man suggested. "But I can help you."

"Yes. I imagine. Help yourself really."

Two soldiers came over to their table. They grabbed the little man by the neck and held him off the floor like a cat. "Scum. Leave this place," one soldier snarled. The stranger was escorted out. Andy and Simon sipped their drinks.

"He could have been sent by the Emperor's lackeys to see what you would say to such a sale," Simon advised.

"How else did he know of all this?" Andy returned.

"He was sent and failed, so he was seized and sent out."

"Perhaps," Andy was noncommittal. "Or he was a lone nothing." The drink was mellowing.

"We are being watched," Simon gestured slightly toward another table. "There are too many people here who suddenly know us."

Andy nodded, pushed away the drink and they made for the entrance. They were outside, looking for a scooter taxi, but a group of soldiers had followed them. "What are you strangers doing in this soldier's bar?" one demanded.

Andy replied before Simon could. "Just a friendly drink. We are outside now and leaving."

"You are spies." The four men came in around them and suddenly there were knives out. Simon reached beyond the knife of one, grabbed a wrist in a twinkling, and sent his man spinning into another. Andy kicked out, then elbowed. One soldier produced a needle blaster. It was a setup.

Andy's first impulse had been to run, to get out and away without a commotion. But to run from a blaster with its automatic sights was useless. Simon threw himself on the man who had pulled the blaster, and while they were rolling, Andy proceeded to kick those soldiers in the head who were trying to get up. He was using the techniques learned at Sanctuary. Only he was not trying to evade now. It was not fair fighting, but neither were blasters against unarmed men.

There was no crowd coming out of the bar. The taxis stood nearby, without moving. The doorman glanced their way and then went inside. It was all going to be decided quietly right here. One kick landed squarely with hard space boots and that soldier was away. The next had a blaster too, braced on one arm, and Andy kicked the arm, and could feel the bone go. Then the last antagonist got to his feet, and he thrust with the knife. Andy was no longer there as the knife swung. Andy struck hard now, angry, he swung again and again. The soldier dropped. The man with the broken arm on the ground was going for his blaster and Andy kicked him in the head as well.

Then he saw the third man, who had dropped his knife, had pulled out a needle blaster. It was aimed at Andy, who was too far away to jump for him or to get away.

Now blaster light shone, once, twice, three times, four. Simon had smashed the man he was rolling with, taken the soldier's blaster and killed them all, including the unconscious ones.

Andy and Simon ran for the scooter taxi stand and ordered a return to the hotel. Simon still clutched the blaster. Airborne, in the stream of force field traffic over the city, Andy asked why Simon had continued firing even at those who did not stir.

The former soldier answered casually, "Dead men sometimes rise to fight again, unless they are very dead. Only in the shows do you settle things with one blow. Even the prizefighters in the ring can not do that. These soldiers were not picking an idle quarrel, but sent to kill us. Their mistake was trying to do it with knives to make it appear as a street incident and waiting too long before taking out the blasters."

Andy nodded. "I suppose it is true."

Simon snorted. "What an assassination crew! One man with a needle blaster sighting us from across the plaza as we left the bar would have been enough. They wanted it to look like it was a mere soldier's quarrel with civilians. Andy, how in the galaxy did you evade them like that? It was fascinating to watch, though I had little time except to glance."

"Some tricks I learned on Sanctuary. Someday I will tell you about that."

Simon nodded. "Now that we know they want to kill us, we will have to be more careful. Safe passage indeed! And then we have an accident! It was all arranged."

"If that's the case, Simon, and I think it may well be, then we should not return to the hotel at all. Our few clothes there are not important. Word could be flashed ahead. Our star liner leaves in the morning, and we can travel the city skyroads until then."

Simon nodded. "They will try to kill us. But it is not yet top priority. They will claim we killed four Imperial soldiers. That will be their excuse for killing us now."

"Which you did, after suggesting that bar." Andy Mars reflected. "Yet Simon, I still believe in you. I suggested we go out tonight. And that was my mistake."

They pulled into the parking slot at the hotel. Andy paid the taxi driver, and then they took the moving pedway down to the hotel lobby. They walked through the long hotel lobby and out another door to the parked private charter capsule cars on the other side. In a moment they were off by private rented capsule, with Andy driving. He had entered enough credits in the slot for a whole night. Andy put the controls on manual to follow a circular route over the city.

They were above the city and Andy prepared to take a nap. Every hour or so he would have to reset the automatic voyage instructions. Simon was right. They needed to be back at the Spaceport at dawn and riding above the city was as good as any way to spend the time until then.

It was hours later when another capsule car pulled up beside them. Andy and Simon were both nodding. They were hailed by a beeping horn and the driver of the parallel car motioned for them to descend to the surface. The other craft held two men, in ordinary costume, but probably officials, military, or police. Andy dropped to the bottom middle lane, then gave it full speed, and pulled away. He could watch everything from the bottom lane here.

"There had to be a lot of checking to find us so soon," Simon declared. "They want a traffic accident now."

"At the speed I'm going, the counters below should notify the airpolice and bring in the barricades," Andy responded hopefully.

"They won't wait for that," Simon advised, looking about.

Sure enough, a blaster hit their car, and they dropped right out of the traffic pattern. Andy fought for control until they bounced, the deflectors still up, five meters off the pedway. It was quite a bounce. At this time of morning the pedway was nearly empty, and they hit no one.

Andy and Simon vaulted out of the capsule; dodging down the pedway as the car above them followed, the occupants trying for a clear shot. Then they were in a building annex, running for the subway.

"Flying about like that was probably too easy to trace," Simon remarked. The subway they were in now might have been fine, but it seemed so uncrowded early in the morning that when Simon noticed the surveillance camera they decided to leave.

Andy and Simon next took refuge in an all night restaurant and returned to the spaceport without incident. Finally the spaceport opened. Inside they were in crowds. Andy was concerned they might be stopped when leaving at immigration control and investigated for the death of the Imperial Soldiers, but that would have created a public incident. They had been granted safe passage. They were allowed to leave the Imperial planet. The ship they took made stops on various Free Planets.

In a Free Planet outer spaceport, they had a ten-day wait for a star freighter back to Eden. The Chalda commerce had picked up enough so that two star freighters a month stopped in Eden these days. Andy used the time on the Free Planet to establish a new bank connection and to set up the first of his planetary agencies outside of Eden for the distribution of the Chalda capsules.

*   *   *

The matter that most concerned Andy Mars on his return to Eden was telling his best wife, Myra, of the wanted poster with her picture on it. Simon needed to be asked to say nothing about Myra. Andy thought about this in the Freeport space station and again on his journey to Eden.

Once they were on the star freighter heading back to Eden, Simon Semple brought up the matter himself while they sat in the lounge. "You are going to talk to Myra?" he asked curiously. "Myra is my business," Andy concluded that topic of conversation before it began. "I ask you to say nothing about what you have seen on the wanted poster. I want your promise."

Simon nodded. "Of course. I do promise."

On his return Andy spoke to John Kent, the former governor who was temporarily running Lorraine while Andy was away. Andy visited Kent in the governor's mansion and they sat on the West Veranda sipping soft drinks. He noticed how old and tired the white haired former governor seemed. Even with men now living to be nearly two hundred Earth years, life finally ended.

"Well, our new leader, how did it go with your visit to the Empire?" John Kent asked.

Andy did not exactly like this epithet. He told Kent of the court room incidents only.

"What do you intend to do?" John Kent inquired.

"If you are able to continue on as governor pro tem, it would be good, because I intend to first try to set up actual agencies for the distribution of the Chalda on all the major planets. The Emperor is right about that matter; the Chalda distribution has grown on its own, like a weed, a wild plant, with middlemen everywhere reaping enormous profits. I wish to set up distributors and extract promises as to prices. The threat will be to cut off sales if they do not follow our price structure. Then I will know who the distributors are and will have direct control. The Empire will pass their laws, but I do not want the overlabeling and the price gouging of the Chalda Elixir to continue either."

"Sure," John Kent agreed. "That way you and the Emperor alone will profit."

"And the planet Eden. I can not fight the Emperor." Andy would not even tell John Kent what he intended to do next. And his travels would be a fine cover story for his buying a star fighter and setting up planetary force screens.

In the late afternoon, Andy Mars left John Kent and returned to his home in town, which was close to the Governor's Mansion. He wanted to see Myra again. Myra, Happy, and Felicity had all greeted him warmly on his arrival.

He asked to see Myra alone. First he inquired about the Chalda production and distribution, which she had been overseeing in his absence. Myra gave her report. She asked about the judgement of the Imperial Court and Andy told her briefly exactly what had happened.

"The most curious thing that occurred on this trip my Myra was to see some wanted posters in Dethilm with your picture on them."

There was a fleeting moment of confusion in her eyes only. Then her eyes opened and closed in a flutter and her lip jutted out in a pout. Finally she spoke: "I have explained all that already before you left. How much am I worth? What was offered for me?"

"It was a million credits."

"Not as valuable as the royal space yacht I stole plus the money I took from the treasury, now spent. My father is still angry and if he gets me back he will still marry me off to someone else. But probably he just wants vengeance now. He would no longer trust me." She snorted. "The question is, do you trust me?"

It was time to kiss Myra's lovely face and return to loving this daughter of the Emperor.

"The Emperor consults many soothsayers, but I have not heard of the Chalda being foretold," Myra declared, as they held each other in bed.

"Simon Semple proved knowledgeable about the Empire, but he also saw your wanted poster," Andy observed.

"Will he talk?" Myra questioned.

"I asked him not to say anything. I can only hope. A lot of credits were offered for your return."

"I don't think Simon would sell us out for any amount of money," Myra replied. "Talking is another matter. I would hate to have questions about my past circulating all over Eden."

12

THE IMPERIAL FLEET: THE FIRST ENCOUNTER

The profits continued to roll in for the sale of the Chalda pills and Andy Mars was off planet more than he was on, establishing agencies everywhere for distribution.

Eden had become a wealthy planet. It was what was called a unitary planet, with one capital at the city of Lorraine and one nation. An assembly accepted a religious national anthem, a flag of green (for the plants) and blue (for the oceans). A road system was begun. Tourists were allowed on planet with a thirty-day visa and an implanted wrist ID tracer chip so they could be found and removed if they did not leave on schedule.

Tall buildings were sprouting in the capital, Lorraine. Builders and contractors came to the planet. Andy insisted that lumber be imported so not many trees belonging to the Great Root would be taken for construction. Another major building material was native stone quarried from the mountains.

Still there were tensions between the city people, the River Rats who now took the increased commerce on the rivers in larger motorized boats, the new immigrants who came in to work in the Chalda manufacturing laboratories, and the Pilgrims.

Some of the Pilgrims accepted working in the factories, but they were upset by the new wealth.

"Their religion requires them to work hard and still be poor," Simon Semple told Andy cynically.

An immigration policy was established to keep to a minimum the number of people who would now flock to the rich planet of Eden. This was easy to enforce, since even now only three space freighters docked each month. Private craft were forbidden. Still there were problems. There was pressure by the newcomers for the Pilgrims to give up their plural marriage to free some of the surplus women. The Pilgrim elders declared that until the newcomers accepted the Pilgrim faith, did penance for a considerable time, and proved themselves, the marriage situation was not going to change. It was a way to postpone the inevitable.

The Chalda pills were being produced by the billion, but the factory was all computerized. Even the Chalda fields of plants growing on trellised vines were harvested with new machinery that plucked the thorns and drained them so no humans would be injured. The fission power plants being installed were costly and Andy Mars saw to it that he had control of the planetary budget. He also began to buy in the arms market.

There was an uneasy peace with the Empire. Agencies could not be established within the Empire, but Andy began to set up offices on many of the Free Planets for Chalda sales. He had begun with the largest, most populous planets.

Luckily Andy happened to be on Eden at the time of the next move in the great galactic game. An Imperial star fighter rolled in, paused over the space dock, and began unloading troops. Andy Mars, Simon Semple, and John Kent met the Captain of the troops at the space dock station.

The Captain was a large impassive man, seeming to fit his silver uniform and epaulets. There was not even a microfighter on Eden as yet, so there was no question as to this Imperial Captain having his own way. "Is this an occupation?" Andy Mars inquired blandly.

"No. We are here on a botanic mission." Almost Andy felt the Imperial Captain was laughing inside at this declaration.

"I see. How may we help you?" Andy asked. Freely translated that phrase "Can I help you" always meant: how can we help you complete this mission and go away. "May I help you?" also often meant what are you doing here?

"We have two botanists on board." the Captain disclosed. "You will show us where you grow the Chalda plant. They will dig some up, pot them, and we will leave. That is simple."

There was no question about paying for the Chalda plants this time, as had been suggested in the high court of the Imperial capital. This was not smuggling, it was blatant theft.

"The Chalda is deadly to those who are stung," Andy reminded the Captain.

"We know that. We all take your capsules and are immune. Even those of us who never took Chalda before, have started to take your pills."

The story on immunity had gone around. Yet Andy had not told this story off planet. Perhaps some of the crew of the star freighter who came through had heard these tales of the Chalda at the Eden spaceport and spread them. Otherwise this sounded suspiciously like information that had accurately reached the Emperor's warriors from an internal spy on Eden. Here was an eventuality Andy had long suspected and feared.

"The Chalda grows wild," Andy began. That was true. It still grew wild in the forests of Eden. But Chalda vines were also being cultivated much in the manner of grapes, on hillside terraces. The area of the farmed Chalda was not large, occupying only two long valleys between the mountains. It was not obvious from the air or even in a survey. Andy would not lead the interlopers to the cultivated fields. He had no intention of making this task easy. He would bring the Captain and his crew to the jungles of Eden and let them take their chances there. That much he could attempt. There was little else he could do.

For a moment he thought of inviting the full crew of the star fighter in for brunch and poisoning them all. But even if they seized the star fighter, it would only be days before the wrath of the Empire came down upon them.

Andy did indeed invite the whole Imperial crew to lunch to ask questions and get a feel of their situation. Mainly they were on a mission and in a hurry.

The Imperial Captain, three soldiers, two botanists, along with Andy Mars and Simon Semple now took a walk into the woods. The contingent was led into the deep jungle. They were wary but followed. Finally Andy pointed out the triangle shaped leaves in a thick grove. "There are the Chalda plants, draped over the trees, their daggers of doom pointed at you. We milk the pods, but we do not dig up the plants. You may dig away if you like."

There was a hierarchy of power here among the Imperial company. The biologists pointed to where they wanted the digging, and the soldiers with mechanized spades began work.

Andy and Simon stood well clear. After a bit the inevitable happened, a tangled vine seemed to dislodge and fall, draping itself across one of the biologists and two of the soldiers. All three men were struck with Chalda Thorns, one soldier right through a space in his armored vest.

The injured men were soon in bad shape and the Captain had them brought back to the ship. Then he returned with a larger component of the crew to dig. Andy noticed the Captain too stayed well back this time, as the digging continued. Eventually the roots of the plant were potted and the vines snipped above.

In snipping, another soldier was struck. He was returned to the vessel while the company searched and located more of the wild Chalda. The third plant potting also gave the crew trouble. Two more men were struck. The way the vines with their poison thorns sprang down was unpredictable. But finally the remaining biologist and ship Captain were satisfied and they returned with the plants to their ship. The next day they were gone. Andy never found out if the injured men survived on not. Since they were all taking Chalda pills the chances for survival was good.

Andy did have a conversation with the Great Root as soon as the Imperial warship had left. "You brought them to the agreed place," the Great Root inquired. "Yes. I thought this would happen. I was sure the Imperial forces would come after the Chalda plants. That was so obviously the next step."

"Then they obtained nothing but totally sterile plants. The Chalda seeds will not grow. Their cuttings will die. The plants will wither when planted in foreign soil. Even the Chalda poison will subtly alter and become more dangerous to use as time goes on. I have seen to that by infiltrating the plants in that area."

"We have won the first round. There are many to go," Andy Mars mused. "Thank you for making the genetic alterations. If I had done it, the trained biologists would have found ways to trace my interference. Your efforts were natural, I am sure."

"Yes," the Great Root answered. "They will believe that the plants just do not grow elsewhere than on Eden, which is what we want them to believe. What will you do now?'

"Now it is time to prepare for battle. I have transferred enormous funds to the Free Planet's banks. I can make an attempt to buy planetary force screens and a star fighter from the Free Worlds and see if we can hold off the Imperial Fleet."

"And what are the chances of that effort being successful?'

"Not good," Andy Mars replied.

*   *   *

So now Andy Mars began what he felt might well be his last life, that of an opponent of the Empire. He set off to buy a planetary force screen and a star fighter, a space craft that was also protected by a force screen with elude capabilities. He was preparing for a war with the Empire, but it would be a defensive war. When the Emperor discovered that the Chalda Thorn plants did not grow and produce anything worth while, there would be a return expedition by Imperial ships to Eden. Andy felt he might have almost a year to prepare, and then the reckoning would come. The Imperial biologists would try many experiments on the plants first.

Andy went to Glaxius near the center of the Free Planets where many things were bought and sold. Shortly he returned with Sam and Sheila Quest in tow, aboard a new star fighter. Sam Quest contacted Hank Greer, an engineer, to install the planetary force screen. Some of the force screen components Andy brought back to Eden himself in his new star fighter. Other deliveries came aboard star freighters in the next weeks. Yes, Andy Mars was preparing for battle with the Empire.

*　　*　　*

Even as the imported technicians installed the planetary force field around Eden, under the direction of Sam Quest and Hank Greer, Andy Mars and Simon Semple practiced with their new star fighter with elude. All were in a hurry. Sam and his sister Sheila wanted to finish their task of installing the force field, take their enormous profit, and get off planet. Andy and Simon wanted to test out and learn to use their new star fighter with its force screen and elude. They maneuvered, practiced feinting, and tested the craft for sub-light speed. How well was it built? How sharply could it take a curve and come about? Every ship had its own peculiarities and this craft was no exception. Since this was to be a defensive operation, they named their new star fighter "the Repulse." The ship had three frontal guns, a laser blaster, a nuclear torpedo launch tube, and a fragmentation destabilizer. The force screen was synchronized to peel back just in front for milliseconds to allow the weapons to fire.

The Repulse sat in a huge newly constructed hanger; eighty meters of star fighter, a cylinder with light cruise power, its fins on the side merely for purposes of steadying the vehicle.

The gray coloring on the vessel was necessary for the elude mechanism, which produced multiple images on enemy screens. It was not camouflage, but a projection of various ships that made zeroing in on the Repulse difficult.

Time passed in an unnatural stillness. There was no word from the Empire. The bureaus set up on Earth and many of the Free Planets to oversee the selling of the Chalda Elixir functioned well. Money was rolling in to the Eden Corporation.

*   *   *

There were, of course those on Eden who disagreed with what Andy Mars was doing. The Prophet asked that Andy Mars come to the courtyard of the new cathedral going up in Lorraine, paid for with the Chalda Elixir. The Prophet, Howard Wenzel, was standing watching the work in progress. The Cathedral would be decades in building because the Prophet had insisted that only stone cutters using ancient tools be employed in the ancient fashion.

The tall, thin, Prophet with his stringy beard that moved either to right or left, but never straight down, now quizzed Andy Mars on this great expenditure of money for defense. Finally the Prophet came out with his problem. "Our original Pilgrim endeavor was to move beyond the Earth so far at supra light speed that we could follow what some believe is dimensionally possible, returning to the actual time of Christ on the Earth. This effort is enormously expensive. We ran out of funds for our venture. We are here now, attempting with the help of the Plant God to set up a new Eden, a paradise, and a beacon for mankind. But with the Chalda money an expedition could be financed with a supra light space yacht that could go back to the beginning."

"You spent ten years in your quest on the Ark before landing on Eden," Andy responded. "Whether what you are talking about here could even be done is unknown."

"Yes, but there are still faster ships now," the Prophet countered. "New break throughs. All of this money is being spent on war."

"On defense against war," Andy corrected.

"And it will only bring the wrath of the Empire down upon us," the Prophet continued as if Andy had not spoken. "Are you really one of us, Andy? What does the Plant God say on this matter?"

"I have not asked the Great Root. You know there is another way and perhaps two other ways. You tried on Mars to use the Time Travel Institute to go back to the time of Christ. You were refused because some in your party wished to prevent the Crucifixion of Christ and weather you are a believer or not, that would alter the time line and at best place you in another dimension. But importation of some scientists and study could furnish us with our own Time Travel Institute right here. That too would be costly, but probably more feasible than using supra light speed. In addition the Great Root tells me that the River Lizards have attempted Time Travel with out of body experiments."

"The River Lizards?" The Prophet was plainly astonished.

"Yes, they are highly intelligent creatures and I have communicated with them. If we survive this attack by the Empire, I will see that your projects are financed."

The Prophet nodded. He had some other things to think about and would leave Andy Mars alone for a while.

*   *   *

The planetary force screen was at last finished, connected to the fission plants for power, and tested. Ships coming in were stopped and searched. The star ship fighter handled like a dream as promised, once the usual kinks were corrected. Sam and Sheila Quest were on the point of leaving.

And then a small Imperial flotilla of five ships arrived with a message from the Emperor.

The Imperial ships were asked to remain outside the force field locks and to state their business. The message was simple. Andy Mars was to return with them to the capital. The Emperor wished to see him.

The entire message was curious. It almost made Andy laugh.

To the Honorable Governor Andrew Mars of Eden:

> Why are you placing a force screen around Eden without Imperial permission and licensing from the Emperor? Why are you holding as a prisoner my daughter, Myra? You are instructed to surrender yourself and my daughter at once. You will come under the promise of safe passage to the Empire and board this flotilla of the Imperial fleet. The illegal Force Screen you have constructed is to be dismantled within five standard days.

Andy replied he was married to Myra, with her consent. He wished the Emperor well, but could not comply with the requests. The force screen was merely defensive to protect the Chalda production. Everyone knew force screens were not an offensive weapon. Andy requested the Emperor to immediately withdraw the Imperial fleet and he instead invited the Emperor to come to Eden himself for a conference. This last invitation was not at all likely to lead to results, as everyone knew. The Emperor was extremely careful of his own safety. He reputedly wore a personal force screen and never left the palace.

Myra also insisted on sending a message to her father, the Emperor, declaring that Andy had nothing to do with the space pirates who attacked her ship. She declared she was happily married to Andy and all they wanted was to be left alone in peace. Since her father desired that she marry the ruler of an important planet, she believed she had carried out his desires in marrying Andrew Mars of the rich planet Eden. The messages were sent by supra light pulse communication so as not to place anyone on Eden at risk. A small craft with messengers might be just seized by the Imperial flotilla. Sometimes the messengers bearing bad news could be killed.

The Emperor's new knowledge about Myra indicated once more that it was obvious someone was sending messages to the Imperial planet from Eden.

*   *   *

There was a conference on Eden at the governor's house in the capital, Lorraine. The new large meeting room was designed to hold what would soon be the beginning of a representative assembly on the planet, elected by all the people.

Eight men were seated about a round table in the meeting room overlooking the river. It was a council of war and they decided to call themselves "the Council." There were the Pilgrim leaders Bishop Jacob Swife and Prophet Howard Wenzel. Next to them sat the leader of the River Rats, Skip Boyton, who was now heading a group of several hundred citizens that passed for an army here on Eden. Skip Boyton thought the Bishop and Prophet amusing and smiled when they spoke. Then there was Simon Semple, John Kent, the old Governor, Sam Quest, Hank Greer, an engineer who had been hired to install the planetary force screen, and Andy Mars.

Hank Greer was a young, handsome man who had been heavily pursuing one of the Pilgrim women. The Pilgrim leaders demanded Hank should join the church first.

The men talked for a several hours about their situation. There were vast differences of opinion.

The religious leaders wanted to send messages to the Emperor and proclaim their loyalty. Bishop Swife proposed Myra be surrendered as a peace offering. Prophet Wenzel nodded agreement. Andy Mars laughed at this and commented: "She is not only my wife, but you good Bishop insisted on marrying us a second time when we joined the Pilgrim community so that we were fittingly a part of the church.

150

And surrendering Myra would only be the first step. The Emperor would not be satisfied with the surrender of Myra alone. He wants the whole planet and next he will be asking the Pilgrims to change their religion and allow only one wife."

Andy was sure that the Emperor did not care about the Pilgrims and their religion. He wanted control of the Chalda plant, Myra and Andy himself. But this gave the Pilgrim leaders something to consider.

"We are being crucified and should resist," Prophet Wenzel snapped, changing his mind abruptly, which was his usual style. "We need a miracle to save us, and one could be forthcoming." The Prophet looked upward and Skip Boyton covered his mouth so no one would notice he almost was laughing.

Bishop Swife did not let the matter rest, however. "The Great Root, which I consider a divine creation, a Plant God or a messenger of hope from the deity, has produced crops on its own, certainly a miracle. It has also placed hedges around the evil Chalda Thorn plants to protect the citizens. And the Plant God has caused many flowers to bloom. This planet is indeed Eden. But the Chalda Thorn is the opposite. It is evil. There is a dualism in nature, good and evil, night and day, rain and sun, man and woman. Opposites. The Chalda has made Eden rich and therefore corrupt and brought the power of the Emperor upon us."

The Prophet Howard now interjected: "The Chalda Thorn elixir makes men feel good. That proves it is evil. Men were made to suffer."

"The Empire is spreading out everywhere," Andy Mars countered. "The Empire is the major evil. It would come here anyway. The only way we can be free in the future is to destroy the Empire."

"Defend against it, you can try," Sam Quest advised. "Destroy it, well it is too powerful. You may be able to deal with it, make some deal."

Andy looked at Sam. "You're saying that in spite of the technological weapons I bought from you, we will ultimately lose anyway."

"Yes." Sam laughed. "But frankly I hoped to be away by then. However I like your spirit Andy. I may actually stay and go down with the ship as they used to say." Sam Quest concluded: "One thing though Andy, four of these five Imperial ships out there now that the Emperor has sent are older warships. They are at least two models lower in scale than your ship. They are ten to twenty years old. True they have been upgraded and fitted with ship covering force screens, probably some years ago. They are larger than your ship, but not more powerful. I've looked at the ships by telescopic viewscreen. The Admiral's flagship alone is nearly new, but not fitted with elude. With luck and skill you can defeat them all. But this is only the opening scene in this drama. After you do what you must, the Emperor will upgrade and retool his entire fleet. Force screens will be added and perhaps elude as well. When the Emperor's fleet returns in force the next time, which they will do, there will be a whole new game."

"Which you don't think we can win?" Andy asked.

"Frankly, as I said before, I hoped to be gone by then," Sam Quest replied.

Skip Boyton suggested the Imperial warships be allowed to land one at a time, and then when their doors opened, they should be rushed and taken over.

"That might work on one ship, but not more," Simon Semple commented.

"Unless we bring the entire crew out under a truce and then shoot them down, it won't work," Andy warned. "And that would hardly be fair. Nor would it be successful. There are maybe thirty officers and crew on each of these ships. Some would come out and then close the doors. If we attacked, they could destroy much of the capital of Lorraine with their nose guns alone if we allowed them to land inside our force screen protection."

John Kent declared that Eden was rich enough now and the Chalda secret should be given up in return for a promise that the Emperor's fleet would just agree to go away.

"They won't believe we are really surrendering the secret now," Andy observed. "They came before and got sterile plants."

Sam Quest glanced about nervously. He was still not certain what he would do. Then he advised: "The planetary force screen is in place as I promised. I was to be allowed to leave at this point. The planetary force screen alone will hold out against five ships. If the entire Imperial fleet comes, seventy or eighty ships, that is another matter. I can not guarantee miracles." Sam looked at the Bishop, as if he was sorry he had used the word "miracles."

Simon Semple, who had practiced with their new star fighter, was all for going out and attacking the flotilla. "Our ship is newer than any in this fleet. It has elude capabilities. I think we can take them all."

"And when the whole Imperial Fleet comes?" Andy Mars asked.

"I don't know about that but we have small craft that could fly up and attach themselves to these warships now," Skip Boyton suggested. "We might break in from above the force screen while you attacked with your star fighter."

Andy nodded. "How can it be that the Emperor knows that his daughter Myra is here?" he asked.

There was silence. It seemed to Andy that Simon Semple shifted uncomfortably in his chair. Andy looked at Simon. The big man was sweating. "Yes, I was in the River Rats bar here in Lorraine," he confessed. "I talked too much one evening. I was asked by some of the men there what transpired when we went to the Imperial Court. My tongue is too loose and should be cut out." Simon bowed his head and appeared very contrite.

"I don't think any of the River Rats informed the Emperor on Myra," Sam Quest commented. "But messages off planet to the Empire can be traced. It is one thing to have too much to drink and another matter to betray us to the Emperor." Andy thought it was nice of Sam Quest to take Simon's part in this matter.

Then Sam added, "But if Myra is one of the Emperor's daughters, she may be a spy here on Eden herself."

"That is possible," John Kent agreed. "I believe those in this room are true, Andy, but once talk begins, it spreads and anyone could betray us. The news of what Simon said could be known far and wide. I am getting too old for all this. Eden was once such a quiet and peaceful place." John Kent sighed. "I was one of the early original immigrants. I am neither a Pilgrim nor a farmer. I am a pre-Pilgrim. I should have left years ago."

"You were always a governor more for the people of the town of Lorraine and the river people than for the Pilgrims," Bishop Swife grumbled angrily, remembering the early days when the Pilgrims came to Eden. "I have talked personally on the big bridge to the Great Root. I agree with the Root that the less government we have the better."

"I never pushed for big government," John Kent spoke softly. "I welcomed you Pilgrims. I even welcomed the Chalda elixir. And I thought it interesting when the pills sold so well everywhere. I did not foresee the wrath of the Empire. But no one did. Or …" he paused.

All eyes were suddenly on Andy Mars. Andy had almost invited Myra to this meeting, but he was glad now he had not. Yes, he had brought the fury of the Empire down upon them with the sale of the Chalda pills. But it also seemed to Andy that the whole group was talking around another obvious problem that he had already stated: how had the Emperor learned Myra was here?

"They have not declared war on us," Hank Greer suggested. "This is an ultimatum, but maybe the whole matter is open to discussion."

"Wars used to be declared back in early Earth history," Andy Mars observed. "There were times it took a year to assemble an army and months to reach the battlefield. So rulers felt they might as well be polite and tell the enemy they were coming since the enemy knew well in advance anyway. It still takes a while to arrive by star ship, but no one knows you are coming until you are there. These Imperial ships are under orders. They are not going to be turned away by suggesting a deal."

Then the lights twinkled for an instant. The meeting broke up for the Imperial flotilla was firing at the force screen. The power on Eden was being put to the test.

*   *   *

Eden's force screen seemed to be holding. The Imperial star ships were applying power at a distance. Andy Mars reflected on the military history he had been studying recently. On Earth, in the early days of gunpowder, the shore batteries could always install larger cannon than the ships attacking. So it was with a planetary force screen.

There were always contests between defense and offense from the time of swords and shields. The force screen was the ultimate defensive weapon. It had brought peace on Earth if not good will to men. But maybe it was that men on Earth did not want to find a way to beat it. If one nation could defeat another country's force shield, then their own could be vulnerable. For a while angry rival groups caused terrorist attacks within countries. This led to travel restrictions. And then at last there was peace.

*   *   *

Sam Quest told Andy privately that he would find a way to trace messages that had been sent from Eden to the Imperial capital. Sam was very knowledgeable when it came to new technology.

Then a light pulse message arrived for Andy Mars from Kalin and the Guardians on Sanctuary. Brian Winthrop was being sent with three star fighters and a contingent of the Inner Circle. The Mystic One was observing all of this from afar. Just how was unknown. They could help, but Andy Mars knew three ships would not be enough against the whole Imperial fleet. Andy felt his whole life was coming together for the approaching struggle.

Still Andy felt it was time to try a combination of the tactics suggested at the meeting. Skip Bolton readied some of his people who had small spacecraft experience. The shuttle-craft and runabouts, scooter ships some called them, held up to four persons. They had no weapons, but they had docking airlocks. Andy Mars and Simon Semple went to their star fighter. It seemed to Andy now that they had bestowed the name "Repulse" on this ship with considerable bravado. But the Repulse's weapons were ready and had been tested.

Hank Greer, the engineer Sam Quest had brought down to supervise the installation of the planetary force screen, joined Andy and Simon. The three men sat in the semi-circular control room of the Repulse, looking out through the triple windows. Greer had volunteered on previous tests. He was good with communications and Simon with weapons. Obviously Hank Greer had his own agenda; he also had expressed hatred for the Empire.

Andy was going to fly the ship. Since their own warship's force screen could not be turned on until they were outside of the planetary shield, it was a little tricky.

As they climbed toward the invisible planetary shield locks for exiting the force field, the five Imperial ships gathered. The enemy would try to get in as Andy moved out. A dozen small scooter craft hid behind the Repulse, flown by River Rats and led by Skip Boyton.

Andy activated the elude and moved unseen through the force field locks. The small craft led by Skip Boyton followed and scattered, once outside the planetary force field. The Imperial star fighters began firing. A tracer cloud was emitted to find the Repulse. The Repulse came in fast, its force field on, pushing directly into one of the Imperial craft.

The two force shields of the opposing ships met and there was considerable bouncing. There was a weakness in the other ship's force shield and the Repulse fired. The firing was simultaneously timed in milliseconds. The force screen at the front of the Repulse opened just enough for a fragmentation blast.

This Imperial cruiser was damaged; its shields went down. The small scooter craft from Eden came in to affix themselves to the sides of the damaged Imperial ship.

Three other Imperial ships rushed in, while the Admiral hung back in his flagship. It was not the first time that leaders had stayed at a distance, awaiting the outcome of events.

Space battles were often over in seconds. The three Imperial warships tried to use their force screen to corner the Repulse and press it against Eden's planetary force shield. Andy wiggled loose, outmaneuvering the larger, but older warships. The Imperial ships were all firing, but their blasts bounced off the Repulse's force screen. The elude made it difficult for the enemy to even get a fix. Several torpedoes went by, fixed on false images and exploded in the distance.

Andy had to somehow maneuver enough to confuse the three ships while Simon tried to wait until one of the ships opened its force screen long enough to fire a torpedo. The first shot was lucky, a weakness in the Imperial ships shield. The next successful blast was pure skill, Simon counting seconds as one of the Imperial warship fired torpedoes and timing the fragmentation blast to enter the opening in the enemy force field at that moment.

A second Imperial warship was damaged.

Abruptly there was a message: The Admiral of the Imperial flotilla was on the view screen. He was a big man in splendid uniform, scowling now: "You have declared war on the Empire and will be judged a criminal, Andy Mars. We are withdrawing, but all of your planet will be destroyed."

The first damaged Imperial cruiser had been captured, taken over by the River Rats from their scout ships. They had pushed in past the enemy ship's damaged force shield and cut their way through the hull at a dozen places. The rest of the Imperial fleet withdrew.

"This looks like a victory, but they will be back in force," Simon Semple growled. "They will outfit their entire fleet with elude and force screens. It will take awhile, but the whole power of the Empire will be brought to bear upon us now."

"How can they attempt to break through a whole planetary force screen?" Andy asked.

"I don't know," Simon replied. "It will be the invincible force attacking the impenetrable fortress. Something will give. The Empire is mighty. They have scientists who will study this problem as well."

Andy nodded. "We can win the initial battles and lose the war," he agreed.

They re-entered Eden's planetary force screen lock and landed the Repulse. Nine of the River Rats had been killed and twelve of the crew on the captured Imperial ship had finally surrendered. Fourteen other Imperial soldiers were dead. Now they had a second warship that might be repaired and outfitted. It would not be enough,

* * *

Andy Mars sent supra light messages out to the major Free Planets. The message was simple. It was expected that the Empire would attack Eden with its entire fleet. Any planet that felt they might be next should strike at the Empire while the Imperial fleet was engaged at Eden. There was at least one advantage to this message in the galactic chess game being played. Some of the messages would be intercepted and it might reduce the size of the fleet the Empire was willing to commit to this project on Eden.

But the replies from the Free Planets were not promising. Why should they risk their liberty in a cause far away? It was a classic case. Andy Mars, who had read widely on Earth's history, thought of the free Greek city-states refusing to unite in the presence of a Persian invasion. Another example was that of the major nations on Earth, way back in the 21st century, so long refusing to unite against nuclear terrorism.

Three warships arrived from Sanctuary commanded by Brian Winthrop. Kalin was calling in the debts that the Guardians had at other planets, but still most refused help.

Andy was pleased to reestablish his friendship with Brian Winthrop, the tall, lanky friend with the square face, almost yellow hair and the curious scars. Brian greeted him warmly. "It is good to see you again, Andy Mars. We have brought three ships. This is not the best use of our resources. We know how to use these ships, but it is not person to person combat. The Mystic One asked for volunteers, and here we are."

Andy hugged Brian tightly and they talked long about the hopeless cause ahead of them.

Three more warships came in from the Outer Alliance. That was all. There followed now this long period of desperate waiting.

Using Sam Quest's connections Andy attempted to buy more warships. Sam did try, but soon confessed: "It's hopeless Andy. I attempted to place an order to buy twenty more star fighters with or without force screens and elude at double the usual price. But the three Free Planets that manufacture star fighters never have these ships just sitting around in quantity. Now the Emperor has forbidden any transactions with you. I fear it is checkmate. Even if we had received some ships, training pilots would be another matter. You are the best-trained space navigator we have. How long would it take to build up a corps of such pilots? That is why you bought a small but extremely powerful ship in the first place."

"Then we will be defeated?" Andy asked.

"I can see no other result," Sam Quest replied.

When you are behind in a game, you can still play the last small cards, Andy told himself. He would pull out the final stops in this hopeless game. He sent messages to the other planets held by the Empire already and told them it was time to resist the imperial dominance. It was time for revolution. Some would inform the Emperor at once in the hope of currying favor. Andy would become all the more a wanted man. Most of the planets of the Empire did not even reply to Andy's pleas.

13

The Imperial Fleet: Space Battle and Defeat

Finally the expected Imperial fleet arrived, some sixty-two ships. Most were outfitted with force screens and elude. They hung well back, a thousand kilometers from the planet, as if to draw Andy's ships out. The Council on Eden watched the Imperial fleet through magnifying viewscreens for a time, trying to determine their capabilities.

Then it was obvious something was being assembled in space by freighters, still further out. A huge series of glass rectangles were being unloaded and attached together, stretching out many kilometers. Soon it was apparent that these were solar reflectors, magnifiers that would direct a destructive light beam down onto the planet. Of course Eden's force shield allowed sunlight to pass through or they would all be in darkness. Once these reflectors were in place, a beam could be focused on the greenery below, the Great Root, the force shield stations, the power sources, or the capital city of Lorraine itself. The glass was curved so the light was not diffuse as the ubiquitous heat panels over Mars, but could eventually be focused and turned into a single heat beam. While these were not the same as the heat panels installed in the high skies over Mars, the effect was soon apparent. The planet Eden's temperature, always stable before, was rising. There was nothing to do but go out and engage the Imperial fleet, hopeless as that might be.

*   *   *

Then at last Sam Quest was successful in tracing a supra light message, not to the Empire, but to the Imperial fleet outside Eden's force shield. It came from the Governor's mansion on Lorraine. This was not what Andy Mars expected. Sorrowfully Andy went over and confronted Governor John Kent alone in his office.

Andy Mars entered the Governor's Mansion and nodded at the secretary both men had used, a pleasant woman who sat in the outer office. He did not knock this time but walked into John Kent's office. The Governor was alone and he arose now, but his face was almost the gray color of his hair. "Hello, Andy."

"Hello John. We have traced your latest message to the Imperial fleet."

"I think Eden's independence is over and we should talk terms to the Emperor," the Governor declared.

"And you would act as intermediary? I think not. This has been going on for a long time. You are an Imperial spy and mole. You are a traitor. Why did you do it?"

John Kent sat back down. "I don't feel any of those names describes me." He looked down. "Why did you sell the Chalda elixir which brought us to the attention of the Emperor? Money, Andy. I was on a retainer from the Emperor. That was money too. I came here to this planet after my wife died, twenty years ago. I was here before the Pilgrims came, before you came, when the River Rats were just beginning to explore the interior. I was here when this planet was just a number, before the Pilgrims gave it the name of Eden. I simply sent reports. I used much of the money I received to buy things for people in the town. I was elected governor by acclimation because of my gifts."

Andy scoffed. "Gifts, bribes to achieve power."

"It was an easy society to live in then before you decided to take on the Empire," John Kent added.

"And you told the Emperor how many ships I had, only one ship with a force screen. That is why when the first five Imperial warships came here they all had force screens. I'm sure the Emperor knows I have eight ships now, with the captured Imperial ship, with those from Sanctuary and the Outer Alliance. The saddest thing for me is your betrayal of my wife, Myra. You informed the Emperor she was here. It's over John. You've done your work well."

John Kent looked down and then he started to arise, a blaster in his hand. Andy was upon him before he could begin to aim. The weapon came easily out of the old man's hand. "I'm sorry it was you, John. It won't be prison, but I want you locked in your quarters without access to communication until this is over."

"It will be over for you soon, Andy. They have sixty-two ships out there. I can still be useful."

"I'm afraid you are out of the loop from now on. The townspeople will not take kindly to this when they find out what you have been doing for years. You will be locked up for your own protection." Andy had John Kent's arm and led him from the room.

*　　*　　*

"We can not just let them destroy our planet. We will have to go out with our eight ships and meet their sixty-two. We do not want the Chalda Plants, the Great Root itself, and the capital of Lorraine destroyed. When our power stations are hit, we will lose the force screen and the Imperial fleet can come in anyway." Andy was talking to the crews of the eight ships they had, the Repulse, the captured Imperial vessel, the three ships from Sanctuary, and the three ships from the Outer Alliance.

There were tactical questions, but the ships were as ready as they could be. Andy Mars looked inside himself. It was introspection of the worst kind. What flaws were there in his character that he had led the whole planet of Eden into this mess? Eden did not need to be rich from the Chalda elixir. The Pilgrims were actually uncomfortable with their prosperity. Most of the profits had gone for a planetary force screen and a star fighter, for war. Now they would be defeated anyway. There was no cavalry coming over the hill to help them. Why had he engaged in this project? He hated the Empire from before his near arrest at the University on Mars. He hated the whole Imperial idea and its malignant spread. Knowing why he had done this did not really help. Still it was important that men examine their own motives.

*   *   *

The small defensive fleet of eight ships took off at night, though three of the Moons of Eden were clearly visible and the enemy was certainly watching. Sure enough, a whole squadron of the Imperial fleet headed toward them, hoping to force the force screen exit lock as they pulled out into space.

The Repulse went first, switching on its elude, and sending torpedoes out in spray fashion set to explode close in. The region was full of turbulence and the rest of Eden's fleet emerged under this cover.

As the defensive fleet all emerged well clear of the planet and into the sunlight now, they fired torpedoes at once at the Imperial fleet. Next long-range torpedoes were fired at the Imperial solar reflector array being constructed. As feared, these reflectors too were behind force shields, but the turbulence bounced them all about, and some were not properly attached yet and shattered. That would only slow the process down.

Then the Imperial fleet was upon them in force, and in a few moments there were a series of dogfights raging. Several Imperial warships came in aiming for each Eden ship. They too had been practicing what to do. The largest contingent, eight ships, aimed at the Repulse. The Imperial ships bounced with the turbulence and one

163

exploded, but there were too many. Six to eight Imperial ships were soon around each individual ship of the Eden fleet. Force screens met force screens and then there was quiescence. They were trapped, like checkers in a corner, with too many kings around them. Once the Repulse went nose to nose with an imperial cruiser, firing first when the enemy force field opened to blast them. The Imperial Cruiser exploded. But then it was all over.

Simon Semple, seated at Andy's side on the Repulse, grumbled: "The Imperial ships have been practicing. They knew how many ships we had. They have many scientists, technicians, and tactical officers. Since we have force screens and they can't shoot us down, they can send in a fleet big enough to smother us, trap us, press us against our own planetary force field on Eden, and just hold so here so we can't move."

None of Eden's ships could move. Space battles as usual were swift. Twelve other Imperial ships, freighters at a distance of ten thousand kilometers continued to reassemble the damaged reflector affray. Soon they would have a ray aligned that could sweep any part of the planet Eden as it revolved beneath them.

Andy stopped fighting his own controls. He looked through his viewscreens. "All of our ships are trapped. Any suggestions?"

"The surrounding ships are so close that if we open our viewscreen even for a millisecond and fire a torpedo now, our own blast will bite us," Hank Greer responded.

"I've wiggled all I can," Andy growled. "There are eight Imperial ships around us. One was foolish enough to fire in this closed in situation and is badly damaged. The rest are just holding us. The communicator light is on. They want to talk; they want us to surrender. I could go into light drive and blow all of us away."

"Suicide would get the eight ships around us and ours," Simon Semple protested. "The odds of combat are good, but I see no reason to die. I am not sure even of our cause. I hate the Empire too, but our deaths would not defeat it."

"They have part of their reflector array almost completed," Hank Greer lamented. "It's finished Andy. There were too many. The other ships in our fleet are awaiting your orders."

Andy clenched his jaw. He pushed the COM button. It was the Imperial Chief of Staff, in a ship far out of the region of combat, who came on the screen. He was a big man, old in years, with a hard square face. "I am Admiral Oliver Dunleaf, Chief of Staff of the Imperial fleet. Do you see how your little adventure has rated to call me here with most of our Imperial fleet? Do you now surrender, Andy Mars?"

"We could all go supra-light speed and take most of your fleet with us," Andy suggested.

The Chief of Staff flanked by two other Admirals was too far back to be involved in such a holocaust and he knew it.

"Go ahead, Andy. Then we will destroy all of Eden and leave."

"None of you will have the Chalda Elixir if you do that. The Emperor will not be happy losing that and two-thirds of his fleet."

Admiral Oliver Dunleaf, the Chief of Staff, smiled.

"I doubt if all the other ships would follow you to Hell, Andy Mars. The ones from Sanctuary, yes. The captured ship with an Eden's crew, perhaps, the three ships from the Outer Alliance, I doubt would follow. We are already dickering with them separately. They and their planets will receive a full pardon if they go home now."

"For how long will they be pardoned?" Andy asked sarcastically. "I was promised safe return on Nelob, and then attacked by Imperial soldiers. I will make a deal. One, I will surrender myself. Two, we will turn off the force screen and allow you a secure landing. Three, I wish to bid farewell to my other wives, my friends on Eden and the Great Root, who is more than a friend. After that I will become your prisoner. The rest of Eden must be spared. This was my battle."

The Chief of Staff thought it over. Then he responded: "I agree. You will have a day to put your affairs in order. Myra, the Emperor's daughter, and Simon Semple must also be surrendered. But the Chalda pill production will come under Imperial control."

Andy looked at Simon. "They can take me anytime, Andy. It is over."

"Simon agrees," Andy answered. "He is a free agent. Myra may flee rather than return to her father. I am married to her but can not speak for her."

"Wives always need instruction," Admiral Oliver Dunleaf chuckled. "Eden is a small planet. Tracer DNA will find her. She can not get off planet."

"Are you a man of your word, Admiral Oliver Dunleaf?" Andy inquired. "This is all going into a pictograph, recorded, and being instantly transmitted out by supra light message to all the major planets, those under Imperial control and those who style themselves the Free Planets. They are free only until the Emperor gets around to them one at a time. But we will see what the Imperial word is worth."

"Yes. You may trust my word. You will be brought to trial, but it will be fair. You have my word on it."

An Imperial trial! That could have only one outcome!

14

THE IMPERIAL PALACE

Eden's force shield was turned off and the small fleet from Eden's home planet landed. Imperial ships then began coming in. As the Emperor's troops poured out, there was an ambush by Skip Boyton and the River Rats.

"Oh no," Andy interjected. He was still on the Repulse. He broadcast to Skip directly. "We have surrendered. Did you not receive my message?"

The return reply was not encouraging. "We can't just let them land unopposed. Skip out." The ground battle was soon over. Skip was trapped and surrendered.

Andy was afraid that now Admiral Dunleaf of the Imperial fleet would use this ambush as an excuse to take punitive action. Nothing further happened until a dozen Imperial Ships had landed and taken secure possession of the single space port on Lorraine.

*   *   *

After the defeat Brian Winthrop with the other Guardians from Sanctuary, Hank Greer, the engineer, along with Sam and Sheila Quest all went into hiding on Eden. It did not appear they were being sought; though Sam feared that if the *Imperial forces traced back the sale of the planetary force screen, he would be in trouble.*

"It is best that Hank, my sister Sheila, and I all hop the next freighter out of Eden as soon as possible," Sam Quest asserted. *"In the meantime there are mountains here on Eden and forests. It will be hard to find us. And the Empire's Admiral Dunleaf is not under orders to bring us back."*

Andy talked briefly to Brian Winthrop. "I am sorry Andy," Brian pleaded. "The Mystic One on Sanctuary predicted this outcome. Kalin and the other adepts were to stay behind. But this was our whole fleet. I do not think you can count on further support from us. I will see what lies in the jungles and mountains of Eden and then try to find a way to take my contingent of followers back to Sanctuary on a star freighter. I have no other orders."

Andy thanked Brian for his help. And Andy knew he did not have much time himself. He must see Myra.

*   *   *

Andy met with Myra alone in their home in Lorraine. "I saw this coming," Myra declared. "I fear for you, Andy. I don't want to go into hiding here on Eden, because they will soon trace my DNA on this planet as the Admiral said. They are looking for me specifically. I will be bundled off to some far planet with a minor ruler to watch over me or perhaps restricted to the Palace. But they won't keep me. I will run again. But they will not kill me. I am the Emperor's daughter, and though he has many children and even grandchildren now, I cannot even keep track of the number, well, he holds tight to all that is his. But you, oh, Andy," she threw her arms around him. "I wish you had never embarked on the route of the Chalda pills." There it was again, the wrong route chosen.

Andy held Myra. He could feel her warm soft body. "We don't have much time," Andy lamented.

"Humans don't ever have enough time. The river lizards are right on that one," Myra agreed. "What ever happened to the old Earth's fairy tales where they all lived happily ever after?"

Myra tried to turn all troubles into a minor joke. Andy went along: "How long is 'ever after.' And what happened in the fairy tales with the man who had three pretty daughters, each more beautiful than the rest? I never could figure that one out. Each one more beautiful than the rest!"

Myra now had her other secret, she hoped, one she would not reveal now. Before Andy left for the final space battle Myra had altered the fertility pills she took and also those that Andy took, a double protection. Myra hoped she would become pregnant, but it was all too early to tell. If Andy was to die, she wanted his child.

Andy said goodbye to Happy and Felicity, whom he considered his two minor wives, in a much shorter time.

*　*　*

The next most difficult part of the task of saying goodbye to Eden was talking to the Great Root. They had a lengthy conversation. He told the Great Root the story of Sanctuary and the Mystic One for the first time. He explained that Brian Winthrop had come to help.

"I see nothing the Mystic One can do that will solve your problems with the Empire," the Root opined.

"Is there anything you can do?" Andy inquired.

"It depends on the scattering of my seeds. The seeds I asked you to take were specially imprinted. They too will want to expand. That was a year ago now. You humans often have trouble with your progeny! I don't know what I can count on." There was this feeling of motion, as if the Great Root was chuckling. "Andy, if you stand next to my sensors with your shirt off I can alter your genetic structure carefully. Any of my plants that survive will recognize you as a friend, indeed their creator. What would the Pilgrims say of my use of that

169

terminology? Would they think it a miracle as the Prophet is always prattling on about when he comes to see me?"

Andy chuckled as well. All botanists and farmers were creators as well as destroyers. He obeyed, taking off his shirt and spreading his arms before the Great Root. This time he felt a tinkling which would have frightened him if it had happened when he first confronted the Great Root. Now it did not matter. He was going to his probable death in the Empire. Nothing mattered now.

The Great Root entered his mind with its telepathic speech.

"Stand close. I am going to change your metabolism slightly."

"Will I have green blood now? Protoplasm?"

"No. Men will not know. You will not know. The new plants will understand if there are any. You will emit an aura. There it is done. The question is did any of my seeds take root where you scattered them?"

Andy could not help his own joking optimism even in the face of imminent disaster. His body felt now akin to having an implanted microchip, a talisman. What hope would it be except more possible communication?

Abruptly there was a blast and Andy was sent flying away from contact with the Root. He looked to the North and saw the triple stems, the thick Great Root Bridge over the river at Lorraine severed, the whole center gone. Andy looked back at the city of Lorraine in time to see the two largest buildings wiped out to the ground by blasters. The Imperial fleet was firing indiscriminately. Now the Chalda factory was hit. Then the cathedral itself.

"Oh my!" the Great Root lamented. "I have been severed. I am no longer one. This is a terrible complication. I may not be able to help you or myself."

"That is the Empire at work," Andy informed his friend the Great Root. "I will say goodbye and I must hurry."

Andy raced back to the city of Lorraine and rushed to a communications building. He soon made contact with the Empire's fleet and Admiral Dunleaf came on the viewscreen.

"Admiral Dunleaf," Andy protested, "We have surrendered in good faith. You promised there would be no retribution visited upon Eden."

"Good faith?" The Admiral appeared amused, sneering, and sardonic. "Your Eden militia has inflicted causalities on our landing party. We have finally put down this insurrection and seized one Skip Boyton, who is our prisoner. Your planet will be taught a lesson. Hold yourself, Simon Semple, and Myra, one of the Emperor's daughters you have kidnapped, in readiness to be made prisoners also. Out." The screen darkened.

Andy considered rushing back to the Repulse with Myra and trying to fight past the Imperial fleet and escape into the void. But even if he could get off the planet the Imperial Forces would trace his warp signature and be after him. It was hopeless. The Imperial fleet stopped firing, but other ships were mapping the planet, landing in many places, investigating. They were in no hurry this time. It was to be a permanent occupation. They would soon discover the planted Chalda fields.

A regiment of perhaps two thousand troops marched, with blasters at the ready, in a kind of parade through the streets of Lorraine. The people of the capital came out to look, but were silent. A contingent of Pilgrims was praying in the main square. The former Governor, John Kent, was released from custody and taken aboard the Imperial flagship. Everyone now saw him as a traitor and his usefulness to the Empire on Eden was over.

Prophet Howard Wenzel and Bishop Jacob Swife were taken prisoners as well as Simon Semple, Andy, and Myra.

Prophet Wenzel was angry that he had to "leave his flock." At the spaceport where they all awaited their fate, the Prophet told Andy: "You and the Chalda Elixir have brought this pestilence upon our people."

Andy did not even reply. In a way the Prophet was right. Still, if he had not tamed the Chalda then the Pilgrim farmers would have continued to die. But of course Prophet Wenzel had not engaged in farming himself. Andy decided that if he were going to be nasty it could almost be said that Prophet Wenzel and Bishop Swife sent others out to die so they could have their widows. But that was not their plan. Andy knew his thoughts were unfair. The Pilgrims had accepted Andy and Myra.

We all rationalize and hate to admit it when we have caused problems. And Prophet Wenzel was right. It was selling the Chalda Elixir in pill form on many planets that had called attention to Eden. Andy felt too gloomy to do more than nod. Everyone, even Myra, had finally gotten around to saying the Chalda Elixir experiment had failed.

At last the bulk of the Imperial fleet was ready to leave. A dozen ships and the military regiment remained on Eden, in occupation.

*　　*　　*

The prisoners were boarded on the Imperial flagship but assigned separate quarters with guards posted at the doors. The trip back to the planet Nelob was apparently uneventful. Even Simon seemed to get into no further trouble, locked in a stateroom with rations brought in to him. Andy missed seeing Myra.

There were no visor windows on the interior cabins of the Imperial star fighters where Andy and Myra were locked in separately. And just where Skip Boyton or the two Pilgrim leaders were, Andy had no idea. All had been strip searched when they first came aboard the Imperial ship. Andy's cabin was not a jail, but rather a basic, secure room with its bed, vacuum washroom, and a wall computer to pass the time. Communication from the ship had been turned off for him and he supposed all the other prisoners.

At last they arrived on Nelob. Then Andy Mars, Myra, and Simon Semple were brought off the star fighter first, escorted by a dozen soldiers.

Again it was always curious stepping off a high ship port onto an extended invisible force screen ramp. A glow had been added here to give the screen ramp some semblance of stability, but still one seemed to be stepping out onto nothing at all with the ground far below. The fact that the force screen was there was taken on faith. The ramp descended to a large door at the space center here on Nelob, the central planet of the Empire.

For a moment here on the force screen ramp Andy was outdoors in overly bright sunlight in Dethilm, the Imperial capital city. Ahead were the vaulting towers of the central city, indicating wealth, opulence, prosperity all based on conquest. Above them was the thick air scooter traffic between the great buildings, riding the invisible lanes of the force fields as he and Simon had done on his last trip to the capital.

Andy heard a commotion behind him and turned. It was Bishop Swife calling to him. "Andy, what will they do to us?" he asked when Andy turned.

"Ha," one of the soldiers interposed: "Fear not religious one. You will not be burned at the stake as a witch." The soldier laughed.

The others were immediately separated and sent somewhere else. An air scooter brought Andy, Myra, and Simon to the scooter pad before the entrance pavilion at the Royal Palace. "Home, Myra," Andy declared.

She nodded grimly. She felt queasy and was sure she was pregnant. She would tell no one, yet.

They were at the main gate now, passing inside the force screen around the palace gardens. Their party entered not by the visitors portals, where Andy had gone before into the formal palace gardens, but they faced the front of the fifty-story light gray stone and marble building with its high turnip shaped domes, Byzantine-fashion, one atop another. The building seemed like a monstrosity to Andy, a travesty of bad taste. It was a mixture of styles perhaps devised by quarreling architects. But Andy knew he was prejudiced. The structure appeared to be a blending miscellany of Versailles, St. Sophia, and the Taj Mahal.

There was a moving pedway through the gardens leading to the main entrance. Halfway there the first pedway ended and they walked through a guardhouse, where the splendidly dressed palace guards in their blue uniforms relieved the star fighter soldiers. The palace guards took over. The prisoners were quickly examined yet again as they passed through a view screen area. Then they were back on a moving pedway, heading for the main entrance, a tall ten-meter high elegant ornately carved door.

This was not the public side of the palace gardens where Andy had scattered the seeds of the Great Root a standard year ago. They were coming in at the front of the palace, perhaps the wrong way for his last hope. Here, just as at the back of the palace, there was also a double row of the tall flowering trees bent in a crescent with their tops seemly connected. The flowering purple trees pointed right at the palace entrance. This effect seemed pretty.

Andy examined the high crescent trees, and to his intense surprise some of these seemed to possess a reddish hue. Abruptly Andy moved off the pedway, easily past the guards, and stood on the thick lawn facing the trees.

The guards were startled by his action, but they quickly left the pedway also. In a moment the guards were back around him. "How did you do that, get around us?" one guard asked.

"Give me just a moment here?" Andy requested. He was standing on the lush lawn beside the pedway, looking at the yellow and blue alternating flowers blooming and the crescent trees with their purple flowers beyond. The six palace guards were opulently dressed in blue gittering clothing, uniforms of authority. Andy, Simon, and Myra had all been allowed to follow Andy and they stood quietly, waiting.

"Sure take a moment," one of the guards agreed. They were not sure of Andy's reception ahead. It was best to just go along. After all it was known that Myra was a daughter of the Emperor.

"He is another religious one. He is crazy," one of the guards declared.

"It is called communing with nature," the Captain of the guards suggested, amused.

And then Andy felt it. There was the communing indeed! The telepathic message came and then amplified. Even the Great Root could not do that. Andy looked around, but no one else received the words.

"You are the creator," came the message. "The one who gave us existence here."

Andy thought hard, not daring to speak: "Yes," he thought.

"Can you understand me?"

"Yes," came the soundless reply. "I am nearly everywhere in the garden now and spreading. I have subsumed. There has not been time to go much beyond the garden as yet. The force screens are a hindrance, but not for roots underground."

"Those in the palace are my enemies," Andy projected a thought. "But what can you do?"

"I have been preparing for this day. You have but to give the orders."

"Come along now. That is enough," the Captain of this Palace Guard detachment demanded aloud.

"The time is now," Andy said also aloud.

"I understand," came the silent telepathic message, an utterance apparently no one else could hear. And then there was a final enigmatic statement from the Plant. What did that message mean? Andy wondered.

And how were these plants communicating? Andy saw no above ground great roots. This was different. The roots must be below the surface entirely.

*　　*　　*

Andy was quite aware that he could have used the techniques learned on Sanctuary and broken loose at any time. The guards were abundant, but not armed. Only where would be go on this planet at the center of the Empire? And now he was inside the force screen of the Palace Gardens and ready to enter the next force screen around the Palace itself. Those screens he could not get through. It would be best to find out what the Emperor wanted and see if a deal could be yet made. Only at that point he would be trapped. Still he would not leave Myra alone to her fate either. It was odd, in songs and poems how some sang of loving someone more dearly than the self. Yet he would sacrifice himself for Myra if need be. The whole adventure was ridiculous. It had all come to nothing.

The palace gates were open. The force screen ahead suddenly receded to provide an opening as they approached and the palace doors swung wide to allow them to enter. They walked into a great mirrored hallway, ten meters high. Andy looked up at massive chandeliers. Ahead was a courtyard.

"This is the atrium, Andy," Myra told him. It was always my favorite place in the palace. It is off limits to all but the select. Fortunately I was one of the select."

The atrium was fifty meters high with a great waterfall on one side and plants hanging from invisible force screens on the other, a cascade of blossoms. Here were the interior hanging gardens Myra had described to Andy once previously. The falling water and the plants caused the inside air of the atrium to be humid. The height of this room made it appear they were all still outside. Groups of young people sat at little tables on the far side sipping drinks while others just sat on the stairs going upward to interior balconies.

Andy wondered where the Emperor's two thousand wives and the ten thousand or more of his children were housed in this Palace. He was obviously not going to receive a conducted tour.

A captain of the guards approached: "You will be given separate quarters until the Emperor can see you," he told them.

"Hello, Stevens," Myra said, smiling.

"Hello, Princess Myra," the Captain acknowledged her. He was taking no chances in case Myra was returned to the good graces of the Emperor. "Welcome back. Sorry you find yourself in this predicament."

"I too," Myra agreed.

"You will be kept in solitary confinement in separate state rooms. You may order food and drink only."

"Do not drink any drinks," Andy told Myra. Myra looked puzzled at what Andy said as the guards led her away.

"You sir, also will have a stateroom," the Captain indicated Andy. "You may also order refreshments," Andy was told. "You will be advised when the Emperor will see you." And the Captain smiled, adding cautiously: "Your warning to Princess Myra was unnecessary. No one in the Palace has ever been poisoned." Andy was led off in another direction.

*   *   *

Several hours passed. At last the door of Andy's room unsealed and opened. Four guards came for him. "The Emperor will grant you the audience you requested," one said.

Andy nodded. He had made no such request. He hoped Myra would be there too. Then he noted that the two guards walking behind him had needle blasters inserted over one finger. These instruments of death appeared almost ornamental. They were meant not to be obtrusive.

The most powerful hand weapons, blasters, fragmentation pistols, destabilizers, or atomizers had all gradually been miniaturized and the kickback absorbed. They could be snapped on a finger, pointed, and fired. The history of many inventions was one of miniaturization. Guns were once so long and heavy men could barely carry them. One true story had survived, the Indians of America being told that the longer the rifle the truer the aim, so the Indians were required to pile furs to the top of the gun to purchase it.

Andy had these thoughts as they walked along. The guards could kill him right now. His options were gone. He had to accept that this was a real audience.

Andy was amazed by the length of the walk down the plush carpets through the marble halls. The ceilings were gilded and ornate; the framed paintings along the walls gave him the feeling of traveling through an art gallery. Then ahead were massive gold doors with highly decorated guards in red and gold uniforms wearing gold colored berets. This had to be it. He would have his interview with Emperor Alexius V and not be murdered just yet.

Andy tensed his body, waiting. He had to be ready for anything. "Expect the unexpected," a friend at the University on Mars had said to him jokingly so long ago. How did you do that? It was a wise old saying, signifying nothing.

The gold doors opened outward toward his group. Ahead lay the throne room. It was an amusing name. Andy became aware of another group of guards coming. Myra was being brought in also. Was that good or bad? He would have to wait and see.

Myra's slender form appeared tiny between the four large guards. She was pale but had a determined look. She held her head high. They all waited.

The room ahead was huge with a high vaulted ceiling. Splendid archaic tall gold candlesticks burned along the side. Someone had read about throne rooms and gone one better.

It seemed to Andy that the theme was that of medieval splendor carried to the absurd.

The room was well lit by the usual muted full wall lights. Goblin-type woven tapestries hung along the walls. Two pike men guards stood beside the throne. The Grand Chamberlain, the king's present advisor, a huge old fellow with a staff and a fez-type hat stood on the right.

Now they were all permitted to walk into the room some ten meters along the red imperial carpeting to the center of the chamber. It was not as ritualized as the ancient Chinese Emperor's kowtow, but there was a required subservience. Ahead the carpeting stretched to spread out over five steps on a raised dais. Some things never changed, Andy Mars decided. The ruler placed himself on a throne above all others, indicating power, position, and control.

The throne was beautifully ornate, its real gold glistened, the carvings of the arm rests were classic, the jewels on the carved legs were probably real. Yet Emperor Alexius V appeared older than Andy expected. He wore no crown, but a bright jeweled diadem on his head that glowed so he appeared to be nimbus born. His long white ermine cloak and splendid velvet robes suggested royalty. His jacket was bright colored velvet with jeweled buttons. He was a real person, but gray. It was not the same image as the picture on the Imperial credits that circulated widely even beyond the Empire to every corner of human occupation in the galaxy. Alexius V's narrow face and sharp nose was not as well chiseled as in his pictures. The Emperor appeared a bit dissipated, gone to seed.

"Kneel," the Grand Chamberlain instructed and the whole group, guards, Andy, Myra did as commanded. Bowing in humility to the enemy. What was the difference so long as he stayed alive, Andy decided.

Andy looked about quickly. There were a dozen guards all along each side of the wall, and every one had a finger blaster. And the Emperor's aura was just a bit translucent. Andy remembered that Alexis V usually wore a personal force screen, so if a guard who was part of a conspiracy turned a finger blaster on the Emperor, the ray would be deflected.

Alexius V smiled now. "All rise," the Emperor allowed. "Yes, we are fully protected, Andy Mars," he indicated, having followed Andy's eye movements that scanned the Emperor's force screen. "I am even in constant touch with those on the planet Eden who are friendly to me."

"John Kent," Andy suggested. "He will have been released. And maybe others."

"Maybe, others," Alexius smiled. His thin lips indicated enjoyment of this situation, while he disclosed nothing.

"You have trained at Sanctuary, Andy Mars. I know of your background."

Then Alexius turned: "Myra, I am disappointed in you, my pretty daughter. You could have had a good life. Why did you run away? You were bright, beautiful, always one of my special favorites."

Myra appeared to go along: "I was one of the inner circle. The select." Then she added: "I was one of the extra special thousand. You were always looking for beauty in women, father. Not the face that launched a thousand ships but the desire that imprisoned a thousand faces."

"Myra, Myra. Some people have talked about having it all. Can you comprehend what 'it all' really is?"

Myra laughed. The guards tried to keep a stolid, solid demeanor, but this was not a usual conversation. No one laughed at the Emperor or engaged in banter. And then Myra added: "You were not a father who had much time for each of his thousands of children. Maybe I ran away because I was too much like you."

"That is a good answer, Myra. It pleases me even. Well, you were to help the Empire by marrying Selwin the Illustrious. He is no longer available. Indeed he has married one of my other more dutiful daughters." Alexius actually paused a moment, thinking, reflecting. "Yes, Clarise was her name. She was a bit more amiable and amenable than you were. But you ran away to live with Pilgrims. We have places of contemplation here on our planet. There is a great cathedral I have caused to be built. And there are religious orders. You will be sent to one such monastic order for a time to think over your ways."

"Get thee to a nunnery," Myra quoted the Shakespearean literature, which was still studied.

Alexius seemed to lose interest in Myra for the moment. "Andy Mars, what shall I do with you?" Alexius was toying now, Andy decided.

Then the Emperor went on: "Inadvertently the Chalda manufacturing plant was destroyed in taking over Eden."

"Inadvertently on purpose," Andy snapped, and then was quiet. He must not show his anger.

Alexius went right on: "That is too bad because it was such a lucrative trade. In a few weeks when the stores of pills in the warehouses on Eden are exhausted the galaxy will be without its pills. We need to restart the operation. There are those on Eden who say the manufacturing facility can be rebuilt. Indeed there are already plans for that. But for some reason the Chalda is not producing when it is harvested. Do you have any thoughts on that problem?"

Andy was startled at this turn of the conversation. Perhaps he was being kept alive until secrets were learned. But he was not sure what was happening back on Eden. He was not even sure what secrets were wanted.

"We surrendered in good faith," Andy stated carefully. "Some of our more volatile citizens arose in an unauthorized and ill-timed revolt. This was easily put down. Again, as I said before to your Admiral when his fleet landed on our planet, the force screen around Eden was purely defensive. You can not win a war with force screens. Our force screen is destroyed now as are our fission power plants. Our one star fighter, the Repulse, was aptly named. It was merely to defend our planet. We can not compete with the Empire. You have proven that. Nor did we wish to compete with the Empire. I offered at the time of the surrender to Admiral Dunleaf to work with the Imperial forces and split the profits on the Chalda pills."

Again Alexius V smiled: "Split. Our split would be ninety and ten for you."

"Even that could be arranged," Andy agreed. "There is profit in the Chalda for all." He had lost the game to the Empire. Now he needed to preserve his life and that of Myra.

"Yes. Certainly you have been out of touch with your former planet for the last nine days of your flight here. You apparently succeeded in growing domesticated Chalda. But it is not the same now. Our soldiers went into the domesticated Chalda fields and they were attacked, many of them poisoned by wicked thorns. And taking the Chalda pills no longer seems to offer an immunity."

Andy was astonished at this, but tried to remain impassive. What was happening back on Eden?

And then as if in answer to his unspoken question, the Emperor continued. "In your Eden forest jungles, Admiral Dunleaf says that there is a colossal plant battle raging. Vines are fighting and strangling each other. The action of these plants is not fast, but the whole planet is in an uproar."

"Perhaps because the Admiral and his fleet were so indiscriminate. They cut the Great Root in several places. There may be a vegetation

181

civil war both above and below ground." Alexius V snorted his annoyance. "Absurd. So it is all the Admiral's fault. Perhaps you want him replaced. Indeed! But I want to know, Andy Mars, and know right now. Do you have an answer to this problem, or shall we just execute you now?"

Myra screamed: "No. We are legally married. I claim Andy Mars as mine. I am pregnant with his child. Your grandchild. Does nothing count with you?"

"Myra?" Andy turned toward her.

"It is true, Andy. Some time ago I fixed the fertility pills."

Again Andy stood astonished, transfixed, and silent.

Alexius laughed. "My grandchild. I have five hundred grandchildren in this palace and a hundred more among my daughters who have married as I commanded them, yes a hundred more on various other planets. You sought to curry favor with me by such a means?"

Myra laughed back, almost in retort. "No. I did not do this for you but because I love Andy Mars and wished something of his."

Alexius considered: "In case something happens to Andy Mars. Well something will."

Andy wondered if Myra telling the truth? Maybe! A child. It was just one of hundreds to Alexius, but it was the only one to Andy.

And then Alexius turned his attention back to Andy: "You have not answered me, Andy Mars. Do you have an answer to the problems on Eden?"

"I would have to return to Eden and talk to the Great Root."

"No. Enough of this nonsense. Admiral Dunleaf wants to cordon off Eden with a dozen force screens. The screens are already on the way with two dozen botanists this time. If there are separate plants battling we will destroy some and encompass others. Do you have a better answer or shall we just dispose of you?"

"I will have to think about it," Andy replied. "This is a new situation." He had no answers and he felt his head swimming.

"So it is new situation for you too, Andy. So you won't be much help. I will not allow you to return to Eden." Suddenly Alexius appeared amused: "In one hour we will have a great formal banquet for Gregory III of the Ponce system. He rules five planets and is here with a delegation. There will be a performance during the banquet and then Gregory will sign papers agreeing to surrender his planets, or I should properly say, incorporate his planets into the Empire. He will marry Nadine, one of my dutiful daughters. I will in turn permit him to rule his planetary system under my command and protection. Andy, you and Myra will attend the banquet. Afterwards we will meet again and you will tell me all you know about this situation on Eden. There is enough of the bargaining. The Empire will control the Chalda production, one hundred percent. I do not haggle with thieves and kidnappers, Andy Mars. If you tell me enough to solve this problem, I shall allow you and Myra to live in a force screened secure place on this planet for the rest of your lives."

"A prison," Myra interjected.

"Yes. And if the information is not enough you will die, Andy Mars."

*   *   *

Andy Mars was separated from Myra again and led back by guards to his locked stateroom, already a prison. Why were they invited to the banquet? Perhaps Alexius wanted to show off his power. But Andy had nothing to offer. Admiral Dunleaf must be sorry for the indiscriminate blasts of his weapons on Eden that had destroyed the Chalda manufacturing facility and cut the Great Root. But the Admiral had probably figured it out all too well by now. The Great Root was no longer one, but battling entities. Force screen enclosures and some botanical studies might actually be the answer if the Empire wished to contain the Great Root. But force screens did not control the battling underground where the separated roots might still fight.

Andy paced about the palace stateroom. Yes, back on Eden he could help. But he had no new suggestions here. If he could talk to the Great Root, even in its present condition, something might be done. Only the Emperor would never allow that. It was checkmate. The end of the game was near.

* * *

Finally it was time for the banquet. The guards came, six of them now, the three walking behind him had finger blasters.

The banquet room was fifty meters long. The table ran the length of the room and was elevated on a dais. Everyone sat on one side of the long table facing out. They were told where to sit. Andy and Myra had five people seated between them, down at the far left end of the table. Simon Semple was still locked up and not at the banquet. He would be under heavy guard.

Seating arrangements at this banquet were almost medieval, Andy decided. In the middle ages on Earth the rulers sat in the center and those of lessor importance sat further away, beyond what was then considered to be the all important salt.

Andy became aware of a large orchestra playing softly at the right. There was a blare of trumpets as Alexius and a young man, who must have been Gregory of Ponce, entered. Being seated near the Emperor indicated which the favorite wives were at the moment, Andy decided. Alexius was still wearing his personal force screen and a hundred guards stood in one line behind the banquet table.

What a way to live, Andy decided. Wear a personal force screen to your own banquet because you trusted so few people. Still the Emperor pushed buttons on his belt and extended his screen out to a whole section of the table. His most trusted wives were included in those around him. The screen was barely visible, a transparent entity.

After Alexius was seated he raised one hand. The trays of food were now brought in, carried by dozens of white clothed waiters. The soup course came first and then the meats, the fouls, the fish, the vegetables, the breads. Andy skipped the soup, the water, and the wine. Something was going to happen and he was not sure what. The secret plant communication outside in the gardens had been not to drink the water. Did that apply to the wine? He had told Myra, for all the good it might do.

The orchestra had been playing Shawn Alexander's splendid "Entrance March" from the last century. Now a spirited conversation began along the table. The young men seated near him asked Andy some pointed questions. The more formal constraints of the throne room were left behind. Andy decided he had been seated surrounded by some scientists, biologists, and advisors. Now Andy felt he had discovered the reason why he had been asked to attend this banquet. They would try to pump him for information.

"What is life like back on Eden?" one man asked.

Andy replied warily.

"Are the Pilgrims on Eden a huge conspiracy against the Empire that should be eradicated?" another balding moon-faced fellow inquired. Andy answered negatively, deciding the Emperor's questioners did not have all the right answers either. They were groping.

The next question was: "How had he first met the Chalda Thorn and talked to it?" Andy replied honestly, "I have never talked to the Chalda Thorn." That led to more questions.

"Why couldn't they grow the Chalda here on the Imperial planet? What was its secret?" Andy replied he did not know.

Andy noticed the Emperor was talking to his visitors from the Ponce star system. It was a conversation break before the show for the Emperor.

In front of them juggling and magic acts began by gifted performers in multi-colored costumes, as the orchestra played.

The dancing girls would be next, for they were ready, standing at the side in elaborate but scanty costume. Andy ate mechanically. He felt almost in a stupor. He was moving toward his doom with no hope. Andy had never felt so completely without a plan.

Some official came over to Alexius and whispered something, but Andy could not hear. Alexius frowned, then shrugged and gave an order. The Emperor raised his wine glass. Andy put his ornate goblet to his lips, but only pretended to drink. He spit some in his napkin.

Abruptly Alexius waved a hand. The whole conversation of the table went mute. "Where is my wine taster?" Alexius demanded. Guards scurried.

In a few moments the wine taster was brought in. He was carried upright by two guards. He appeared to be unconscious or worse, his head lolling to one side.

"Gregory of Ponce," Alexius explained. "This is not our usual situation. I have contacted my fleet, which still patrols our planet. We are secure, but somehow we are under attack."

Gregory of Ponce, a droll little fellow with a strange smile seemed a bit unsettled. "It is not me, oh great Emperor. I arrived here with but a single ship, which is still circling behind the planetary force screen." Gregory next clasped the arm of the pretty young girl beside him. "In addition," he added, "having talked to your daughter, I am quite satisfied with my bride to be. But there are oddities that probably should not be mentioned at a banquet. However, I am accustomed to better things. I reported, of all matters, that the toilets in my suite of rooms are not working, and no one could seem to get them fixed."

"It's all over the palace," a man further down the table declared. "The plumbing is not in order."

Just then several people at the banquet table seemed to pass out, several dropping their heads right down in their plates.

"Grand Chamberlain, guards, investigate," Alexius demanded.

"The kitchen staff is all asleep," declared the Grand Chamberlain. He had been back looking already. "Drugged perhaps."

And then Emperor Alexius V fell out of his large chair to the floor. His personal force screen made his position even more grotesque for his legs came up.

The Grand Chamberlain, a massive fellow with a great flowing robe, a splendid red gown, and a long staff strode over to Andy Mars: "What do you know of this?" he demanded.

"I have been watched every minute since I have been here," Andy retorted. Gregory of Ponce fell over as well at this moment. Almost all that sat at the long banquet table were now asleep or worse. Andy hoped it was just drugged sleep. Myra and a few others who had not tasted the wine remained sitting upright at the banquet table.

"You were seen stopping in the garden," the Grand Chamberlain indicated. The Chamberlain had been standing at the side, watching, and had consumed no wine or water.

"Do you perhaps know that the outer force field around the garden has also malfunctioned? There are furthermore an enormous number of seeds blowing in the wind to the city outside of the garden. That is not usual. There seems to be a growth of roots and vines in our electrical circuitry and in our plumbing. You are a plant man. A botanist. Tell us Mr. Andy Mars, the botanist, what is happening?"

Andy shrugged. "I know not. So the force screen around the gardens is off. How goes the force screen around the palace?"

"It too is malfunctioning. But this is all planned somehow. The palace force screen we can not even turn off for the moment. It seems locked, frozen. We are all trapped in the palace until we can get it fixed. The situation is being investigated. Now, tell me what you know."

Several messengers came in to talk to the Grand Chamberlain. He beckoned to the guards. "Don't stand there at attention like fools. Help your Emperor out of this room and to bed. Call some doctors. Andy Mars, I will have you killed right now if I can not solve this problem. I am getting in reports from all over. Toilets," he scoffed. "Pipes are being strangled everywhere in the palace. People are passing out from the water as well. Yet you are unaffected! Why? Answer me now." The Chamberlain brought a small finger blaster out of a robe pocket and pointed it directly at Andy.

"You are unaffected too. Maybe it is you?" Andy suggested.

"I have had nothing to eat or drink and been watchful," the Chamberlain declared angrily.

"If you kill me, you will all die in here," Andy replied. He did not know this, but it seemed a good bluff. It was a time for bluff. "What is your name, Grand Chamberlain?"

The Grand Chamberlain flushed. "Baldwin is my given name. I have ordered the army to send a contingent and take over the garden. We will see what flame throwers and blasters do to your plants."

Andy remembered at this time, almost curiously, that the Great Root on Eden had divulged that it could feel no pain when attacked.

"You will only destroy the Emperor's garden without result, Baldwin," Andy divulged. "And the Emperor will not thank you for that."

"Then you are responsible. You know of this?" The Chamberlain made a threatening wave with his weapon.

"Yes, Baldwin. Killing me will cause you all to be destroyed. Let us awaken the Emperor. Take me, yourself, Myra, the Emperor and as many guards as you like to the Central atrium where the plants are cascading down. We can awaken the Emperor and discuss this rationally." Another bluff. Could the Emperor be awakened? Some of the soldiers behind them who had had a drink of water before coming on duty were teetering. Others fell over. The whole line of guards was in disarray.

"Oh, you wish to go to the center of the conspiracy." The Chamberlain laughed. "You want to visit your plants."

Then the entire room shook briefly. A jagged crack appeared zigzagging across the floor. Some of the great columns had a crack as well. The chandeliers swayed. The dancing girls, who had been waiting at the side began screaming and ran from the banquet hall. They were plainly frightened.

The Chamberlain was now obviously unnerved. He was accustomed to giving information to the Emperor, being watchful and awaiting orders. He was loyal to the Emperor, though he had not disclosed to his majesty some of the machinations of the Emperor's heir apparent, the Prime Son, Justin. The old plots for a coup by Justin had been secretly foiled. The Emperor was not told.

"Guards," Baldwin ordered. "Drink no more water. Those of you not feeling well, you may sit or lie down. Those still able to do so, go fetch the Emperor on a chair. Fetch the Emperor's bodyguard, if any can be found. We will go to the atrium."

The building shook again.

Baldwin tried for a voice of authority: "Some of you guards, ah Captain Stevens, you are still standing. Take charge of a contingent and consult with the engineers. See what is happening to the palace. The building is being shaken to the foundations, and except for the three floors below ground levels, this is the foundation. When you know something, send back a report to me in the atrium as soon as possible."

Stevens nodded uncertainly and left. Someone always stepped into a power vacuum. Stevens felt he should really be Grand Chamberlain. This was not being handled well. Yet Stevens obeyed orders, for now.

Baldwin, the Grand Chamberlain, now turned to Andy Mars. "The Emperor's Prime Son, Justin, is also unconscious at his banquet place, as are our visitors from Ponce. They are not responsible for this. So Andy Mars, it is you. Still blasters work." Baldwin raised his weapon and fired a test blast at the side of the wall. There was smoke and a large hole. "You better have a solution," the Chamberlain added.

Just then the lighted iridescent walls flickered, once, twice, and abruptly the whole banquet hall was dark except for the candles on the table and at the side of the room.

Baldwin seemed to come unstuck for a moment, and then he ordered: "Get many more candles. Come, we will go to the atrium," Fortunately the palace was archaically loaded with candles many on great gold candlesticks.

*   *   *

The Atrium, with its cascading water and massively high plants held by force screens, was now lit by a hundred huge candles in ornate holders at the side of the room. The Emperor was carried in, and placed on a chair. Carrying the Emperor and placing him down on a chair had been tricky with the force screen still on. "What happens now, Andy" Myra whispered.

"I don't know either. We will see," he replied, also whispering.

189

"Clear the rest from this room except for this group," Baldwin the Grand Chamberlain demanded. The curious and those sitting at the little tables on the side of the room left quickly. Baldwin looked up at the dozens of balconies with other people above peering over.

"You all return to your rooms and do not drink the water," the Chamberlain ordered.

Then Baldwin took out his blaster and aimed at one of the thick cascading plants climbing skyward. He fired a burst and a section of the plant turned dark. There was a smell of smoke in the air. Again the palace shook as if in response. Then the great waterfall ceased flowing. There was a murmur among the guards.

Now Andy spoke: "Oh Plant God, can we revive the Emperor, please. I wish to talk to him."

Andy had no idea if plants had moods. Would this plant be angry that some of its foliage had been blasted? He was not even sure he could communicate from here, inside the Palace, with these plants in the hanging gardens of the atrium. Yet roots could run deep. Seeds from the Palace garden could have been brought in clinging on clothing.

And then in answer Andy received the directed message from the plant, which suddenly all in the room could hear inside their heads: "Strip the clothes from the Emperor and bring him right up to me." Here was the Plant's reply. The Emperor without clothes, just as in the old fairy stories! Andy wondered if he could get away with that. He would have to make his demands strong.

"You called it a Plant God," the Grand Chamberlain Baldwin observed pointedly. "On your planet, Eden, I have heard that is what some large plants are called by the Pilgrims there."

"Yes. The Plant Gad has spoken to all of us."

"Spoken," Baldwin scoffed. "I have heard, but what is it?"

"Communicated then. Ordered. Demanded. The only way to revive the Emperor is to turn off his force screen, strip him naked and bring him over next to the plants here."

Baldwin was incredulous. "Naked. That is absurd."

"I will not be responsible unless you carry out this order."

"Order?" Baldwin seemed reduced at last to one word responses.

"Yes. I will take full blame for this action. But we must hurry. Now. Move." Giving the matter a sense of urgency would probably be the most successful.

Baldwin literally jumped: "I don't know if I can even turn off his force screen."

The Emperor's personal screen was rather special, encompassing his body and going to the floor. Yet it was capable of being extended to enclose other objects by touching his belt. Baldwin had watched many times as the Emperor operated the controls of his personal force screen from his belt. Now the Emperor was sitting on a chair with his feet on another chair. Baldwin reached under the raised screen to the belt. He pushed a button. The slight glow of the screen switched off.

Baldwin spun quickly and aimed his blaster at Andy. There were at least twenty other guards in the room, some with finger blasters.

"Guards," Baldwin commanded, point your weapons at this man. Now, you two guards come over here and help me unclothe the Emperor. Quick. You two." He pointed.

The guards did not like their assignment. They came over reluctantly and Baldwin directed them. The Chamberlain did not want to be caught with his hands on the Emperor's person in case the ruler awakened. "Is this really necessary?" Baldwin asked in the middle of the activity.

"The Plant God commands it, or the Emperor will die," Andy growled.

"Then all those at the table will die too?" Baldwin asked.

"The Plant God is mostly angry with the Emperor," Andy responded.

Just then two messengers came in at a dead run. "Halt," Baldwin demanded. "Why this unseemly haste?"

The guards slowed down and came over to talk the Chamberlain in private.

"Speak so we may all may hear," Andy Mars commanded.

The guards appeared uncertain. Baldwin nodded affirmatively.

"We are reporting on what the Grand Chamberlain sent us to observe," one of the guards spoke quickly. "We are told that in the second subbasement, the engineering quarters, the outside water supply, and the electrical system is all buckling up. The masonry is cracking. There are great vines growing into the equipment. Electrical cables are being crushed. The engineers are awaiting your orders to blast these vines. They have hesitated because it is uncertain what affect that will have on the palace building itself. The Chief Engineer is talking about the plant undermining the foundations of the Palace. Undermining. Is that like mining?"

The guard who spoke was certainly confused. He was suddenly aware of the half-dressed condition of the Emperor and fell silent, his mouth open.

"No, fool," Baldwin snarled. "He means undermining the building."

"Do nothing now," it was Andy Mars who spoke. "Wait over there with the other guards. You two, finish with your Emperor first."

Alexius splendid velvet robes and white ermine cloak lay neatly folded on the floor. The high-necked jacket with the jeweled buttons followed. The guards finished at last with the underwear and held up the tall, thin figure of Alexius V, stark naked.

"We will all be killed for viewing this," a guard in the background suggested fearfully.

Indeed Alexius V was not so imposing now; he appeared even scrawnier naked.

"No. The Emperor will thank us for restoring him," Andy informed them all. "Now, carry the Emperor over to this first cascade of plants."

The guards obeyed. Baldwin stood, shaking nearby. "Closer," Andy demanded.

Andy could hear the plant communicating only inside his head now. "You are not being coerced, Andy Mars, my creator, but do you really want to restore the Emperor to consciousness?" the plant inquired.

"Yes, bring him back to consciousness now. I would like to talk to him." Andy spoke aloud so that all might hear that side of the conversation.

"Then hold out his arms and bring him forward until he makes contact." The plant spoke to all in the room inside their heads.

A limp arm of the Emperor had been placed on each guard's shoulder and they moved him right up to the lush plants with their great green many pointed leaves. Alexius seemed to twitch, then stir.

Baldwin opened his mouth to speak, but Andy motioned and cut him off. "Hold him still and right up to the plant."

Andy was receiving and sending new silent communications to and from the plant. The situation was even more under control than Andy would have imagined.

Abruptly Alexius V opened his eyes. He pulled clear of the guards with an effort, and then tottering, leaned on them. Andy felt the fear of all the people about him in the room.

"What is happening?" Alexius demanded, looking down, seeing his nakedness. "Is this a coup?" His worst fears were exposed.

"Yes," Andy declared. "You must surrender now or the Plant God will inflict pain. Soldiers, he is weak. Do not let him fall." The fearful soldiers held tight to the Emperor's arms.

Alexius looked about. "Why is it so dark in here?"

"The power is off. The water is off. The Palace itself can be brought down." Andy laughed. "You are a prisoner in your own house."

"I have a whole war fleet," Alexius grumbled weakly.

"The force screen of the palace is turned on and locked down," Andy explained. "Your own fleet can not get to you without destroying you and your palace." Andy now turned to the Grand Chamberlain and the remaining guards. "Drop your weapons or the plant will kill your Emperor. Do as I say or you will all die. NOW!"

Most of the guards dropped their weapons. Some looked at the Grand Chamberlain for orders. The situation was still sticky, touch and go.

Then Andy smelled the perfume, the sweetness of the plant flowers, permeating the air, a clinging odor. The guards were not all going to listen. Above him Andy Mars saw a glint of weapons from the balcony.

It was time to use the skills learned in Sanctuary.

Andy swung back past the Grand Chamberlain, maneuvering, moving too fast to be a good target, and the soldiers were falling now, the sweet knockout gas of the plant was spreading everywhere. Even Myra looked puzzled and then she simply keeled over. Some people were coughing, staggering. People collapsed in various ways. Some attempted to run from the room, pulling a shirt up over their nose and mouth. But the paralyzing perfume was everywhere now, in the ventilation system, moving through the whole Palace.

The Grand Chamberlain rushed Andy with his staff held high and then fell in a heap. The guards dropped the Emperor who looked startled and then was once more no longer conscious. Two guards fell from an upper balcony, leaning over for a shot at Andy and then passing out. They were the only permanent casualties. The scent of the flowers was moving everywhere in the palace.

At last Andy paused, tired from moving so fast. He was the last man standing. He alone was unaffected by the subtle plant perfume due to the change in his genetic structure by the Great Root.

Andy sat down amid the chaos. It was over. No one was stirring. Yet they were still alive, breathing, though some were gasping a bit.

*   *   *

In a few minutes Andy Mars would walk over to the cascade of plants that had brought the Empire down, here at the royal palace at its very center. He would communicate at length with this "Plant God" and determine what to do next.

Right now Andy was breathing only heavy sighs of relief. In a little while, when the air cleared, he would pick up Myra and bring her to the plant to be revived first. Next he would go to the twice fallen naked Emperor Alexius V and hold him up for revival before the plant.

Finally, before anyone else was awakened, the three of them, Andy Mars, Myra his pregnant wife, and her father, Emperor Alexius V, would have a very private chat about the future of the Empire and the galaxy.

A few minutes ago his whole life had passed before Andy Mars, much as a drowning man is supposed to view his past. Andy had reflected instantaneously on his student days on Mars, on his time as the navigator of the great star ships, then as the pilgrim farmer on Eden, and finally as the merchant prince selling the Chalda Elixir to the whole galaxy.

Now he would live on to still other possible lives he could not yet imagine.

TIME TABLE

Earth
Living & Space Population Government

2000 A.D. 1. Explore solar system 6 billion World Federation
2. Colonize Moon, Mars, 12 billion 300 nations
Jupiter's Moons
Mining operations
3. Successful fusion
4. Nuclear wars
5. Life extension techniques begin

2200 A.D. 1. Exploring probes to 14 billion Beehive living nearby stars begin
2. Begin manned flight to nearby stars by suspended animation
3. Unlimited power leads to cheap distilled water from the oceans. Earth's deserts become gardens.
4. Force screens maintain world peace

2300 A.D. 1. Star Drive 20 billion – female domination (300 A.S.A.)
Colonization of 17 billion males nearby stars begins 3 billion females
2. Robot workers Great exodus from Earth
3. Artificial humans – begins some passing as people.
4. Great artificial oceanic islands built on Earth to produce food.

2400 A.D. 1. Climate control on Earth 30 billion population (400 A.S.A.) 2. Improved light drive starships reach distant suns
3. A whole quadrant of the Galaxy is explored.
4. The Empire is established in the out worlds

2500 A.D. Future time of this story – 50 billion people living on (500 A.S.A.) Earth and billions more on star systems beyond.
A.S.A. = After the Space Age. Severe population control on Earth.

TRUE DIRECTIONS
An affiliate of Tarcher Perigee

OUR MISSION

Tarcher Perigee's mission has always been to publish
books that contain great ideas. Why? Because:

GREAT LIVES BEGIN WITH GREAT IDEAS

At Tarcher Perigee, we recognize that many talented authors, speakers,
educators, and thought-leaders share this mission and deserve to be published –
many more than Tarcher Perigee can reasonably publish ourselves. True
Directions is ideal for authors and books that increase awareness, raise
consciousness, and inspire others to live their ideals and passions.

Like Tarcher Perigee, True Directions books are designed to do three things:
inspire, inform, and motivate.

Thus, True Directions is an ideal way for these important voices to
bring their messages of hope, healing, and help to the world.

Every book published by True Directions– whether it is non-
fiction, memoir, novel, poetry or children's book – continues
Tarcher Perigee's mission to publish works that bring positive
change in the world. We invite you to join our mission.

For more information, see the True Directions website:

www.iUniverse.com/TrueDirections/SignUp

Be a part of Tarcher Perigee's community to bring positive change in this
world! See exclusive author videos, discover new and exciting books, learn
about upcoming events, connect with author blogs and websites, and more!
www.tarcherbooks.com

TRUE DIRECTIONS
AN AFFILIATE OF TARCHER PERIGEE

Printed in the United States
By Bookmasters